Love, etc

Love, etc

JULIAN BARNES

JONATHAN CAPE
LONDON

Published by Jonathan Cape 2000

2 4 6 8 10 9 7 5 3 1

Copyright © Julian Barnes 2000

Julian Barnes has asserted his right under
the Copyright, Designs and Patents Act 1988 to be identified
as the author of this work

First published in Great Britain in 2000 by
Jonathan Cape
Random House, 20 Vauxhall Bridge Road,
London SW1V 2SA

Random House Australia (Pty) Limited
20 Alfred Street, Milsons Point, Sydney,
New South Wales 2061, Australia

Random House New Zealand Limited
18 Poland Road, Glenfield,
Auckland 10, New Zealand

Random House (Pty) Limited
Endulini, 5A Jubilee Road, Parktown 2193, South Africa

The Random House Group Limited Reg. No. 954009

A CIP catalogue record for this book
is available from the British Library

ISBN 0-224-06109-7

Papers used by The Random House Group Limited are natural,
recyclable products made from wood grown in sustainable forests;
the manufacturing processes conform to the environmental
regulations of the country of origin

Typeset by Deltatype Ltd, Birkenhead, Merseyside
Printed and bound in Great Britain by
Mackays of Chatham PLC

to Pat

1 : I Remember You

Stuart   Hello!

We've met before. Stuart. Stuart Hughes.

Yes, I *am* sure. Positive. About ten years ago.

It's all right – it happens. You don't have to pretend. But the point is, I remember you. *I* remember *you*. I'd hardly forget, would I? A bit over ten years, now I come to think of it.

Well, I've changed. Sure. This is all grey for a start. Can't even call it pepper-and-salt any more, can I?

Oh, and by the way, *you*'ve changed too. You probably think you're pretty much the same as you were back then. Believe me, you aren't.

Oliver   What's that companionable warble from the neighbouring wankpit, that snuffle and stamp from the padded loose-box? Could it be my dear, my old – old as in the sense of former – friend Stuart?

'I remember you.' How very Stuart. He is so old-, so former-fashioned that he likes naff songs which actually predate him. I mean, it's one thing to be hung up on cheap music synchronous with the primal engorgement of your own libidinous organs, be it Randy Newman or Luigi Nono. But to be hung up on the sun-lounger singalongeries of a previous generation – that's so very, so touchingly Stuart, don't you find?

Lose that puzzled expression. Frank Ifield. 'I Remember You.' Or rather, I remember yoo-oo,/ You're the one that made my dreams come troo-oo. Yes? 1962. The Australian yodeller in the sheepskin car-coat? Indeed. Indeedy-doo-oo. And what a sociological paradox he must have represented. No disrespect to our bronzed and Bondi'd cousins, of course. In the world's fawning obeisance before every cultural sub-grouping, let it not be said that I have anything against an Australian yodeller *per se*. You might be one yourself. If I prod you, do ye not yodel? In which case, I would give you honest eye-contact and an undiscriminatory handshake. I would welcome you into the brotherhood of man. Along with the Swiss cricketer.

And if – by some happy whim – you actually are a Swiss cricketer, an off-spinner from the Bernese Oberland, then let me just say, simply: 1962 was the very year of the Beatles' first revolution at forty-five turns per minute, and Stuart sings Frank Ifield. I rest my case.

I'm Oliver, by the way. Yes, I know you know. I could tell you remembered *me*.

Gillian   Gillian. You may or may not remember me. Is there some problem?

What you have to understand is that Stuart wants you to like him, needs you to like him, whereas Oliver has a certain difficulty imagining that you won't. That's a sceptical look you're giving me. But the truth is, over the years I've watched people take against Oliver and fall under his spell almost at the same time. Of course, there've been exceptions. Still, be warned.

And me? Well, I'd prefer you to like me rather than the reverse, but that's normal, isn't it? Depending on who *you* are, of course.

Stuart   I wasn't actually referring to the song at all.

Gillian   Look, I actually haven't the time. Sophie's got music today. But I've always thought of Stuart and Oliver as opposite poles of something . . . of growing up, perhaps. Stuart believed that growing up was about fitting in, about pleasing people, becoming a member of society. Oliver didn't have that problem, he always had more self-confidence. What's that word for plants which move in relation to the sun? Helio something. That's what Stuart was like. Whereas Oliver –

3

Oliver   – was *le roi soleil*, right? The nicest spousal compliment I've had in some time. I've been called some things in this sublunary smidgeon which goes by the name of life, but King Sol is a new one. Phoebus. Phoe-Phi-Pho-Phumbus –

Gillian   – *tropic*. Heliotropic, that's the word.

Oliver   Have you noticed this change in Gillian? The way she puts people into categories? It's probably her French blood. She's half French – you remember that? 'Half French on her mother's side': that ought to mean quarter French, logically, don't you think? Yet what, as all the great moralists and philosophers have noted, has logic got to do with life?

Now, had Stuart been half French, in 1962 he would have been whistling Johnny Hallyday's Gallic version of 'Let's Twist Again'. That's a thought, isn't it? A pungent *pensée*. And here's another: Hallyday was half Belgian. On his father's side.

Stuart   In 1962 I was four years old. Just for the record.

Gillian   Actually, I don't think I do put people into categories. It's just that if there are two people in the world I understand, they're Stuart and Oliver. After all, I have been married to both of them.

Stuart   Logic. Did someone use the word? I'll give you logic. You go away, and people think you've stayed the same. That's the worst piece of logic I've come across in years.

Oliver   Misprise me not about *les Belges*, by the way. When some jaunty little dinner-table patriot ups and demands 'Name me six famous Belgians', I'm the one with his hand in the air. Undeterred by the words 'Apart from Simenon'.

It may not be to do with her being French at all. It could be middle-age. A process that happens to some, if not necessarily all of us. With Gill the train is coming into the station roughly on time, steam activating its beloved whistle and the boiler a tad hot and bothered. But ask yourself when Stuart became middle-aged and the only area for debate is whether it was before or after his testicles descended. Have you seen that photo of him in his pram wearing a little three-piece suit and pinstripe nappies?

Whereas Oliver? Oliver long ago decided – no, knew instinctively – that middle-age was infra dig, *déclassé* and generally below the salt as a condition. Oliver is planning to compress middle-age into a single afternoon of lying down with a migraine. He believes in youth, and he believes in wisdom, and plans to pass from wise youth to young wisdom with the help of a palmful of paracetamol and an eye mask from some exotic airline.

Stuart   Someone once pointed out that you can recognise a complete egomaniac by the way they refer to themselves in the third person. Even royalty doesn't use the royal plural any more. But there are sportsmen and rock stars who talk about themselves like that, as if it was normal. Have you noticed? Bobby So-and-So's accused of cheating, to win a penalty or something, and he replies, 'No, that's not the sort of thing Bobby So-and-So would do.' As if there's some separate figure out there, under the same name, taking the flak, or shouldering the responsibility.

Which is hardly the case with Oliver. You couldn't exactly call him famous, could you? Yet he refers to himself as 'Oliver', as if he was an Olympic gold medallist. Or a schizophrenic, I suppose.

Oliver   What do you think of North–South debt restructuring? The future prospects of the euro? The smile on the face of the tiger economies? Have metal traders exorcised the ghost of the meltdown scare? I'm sure Stuart has robust and portly opinions on all such matters. He will be not so much grave as positively gravid. I'll bet you six famous Belgians he doesn't know the difference between the two words. He's the sort of person who expects the word *gravid* to be followed by *lax*, silly old fishface that he is. A billboard for probity, and all that. But a little, shall we say, lacking in irony?

Gillian   Look, stop it, you two. Just stop it. This isn't working.
  What sort of impression do you think you're giving?

Oliver   What did I tell you? The train is coming into the station, puff puff, huff huff . . .

Gillian   If we're getting into this again, we have to play by the rules. No talking amongst ourselves. Anyway, who's going to take Sophie to music?

Oliver   Gillian, in case you're wondering, is an honorary representative of The Men Who Guess.

Stuart   Are you interested in pork? Real pork, with real taste? Where do you stand on GM?

Oliver   Six, apart from Simenon? Easy-peasy. Magritte, César Franck, Maeterlinck, Jacques Brel, Delvaux and Hergé, creator of Tintin. Plus fifty per cent of Johnny Hallyday, I add as a *pourboire*.

Gillian   Stop it! You're as bad as one another. No-one knows what you're talking about. Look, I just think we ought to expl*ain* things.

Stuart   As bad as one another. That's open to question, I think. In the present circumstances.

All right, I'd like to explain something. Frank Ifield actually wasn't an Australian. He may have lived there, but he was born in England. Coventry, if you must know. Also, while we're on the subject, 'I Remember You' was in point of fact a Johnny Mercer song written twenty years previously. Why do culture snobs always sneer about things they're completely ignorant of?

Oliver   *Explain* things? Can't we leave that until we reach the Dies Irae, until some hydra-cocked Pandaemonian prods us with his dipstick and a bat-headed lizard unwinds our guts on a windlass? Explain things? You really think we ought? This isn't daytime TV, let alone the Roman Senate. Oh, very well, then. I'll go first.

Stuart   I don't see why he should. That's absolutely typical Oliver. Besides, everyone in marketing knows it's always the first story that sticks in the mind.

Oliver   Baggies I first. Baggies baggies *baggies*.

8

Gillian   Oliver, you're forty-two. You can't say baggies.

Oliver   Then don't smile at me like that. Baggies. Baggy baggy baggy and another baggy. Go on, give us a laugh. You know you want to. Please. Pretty please.

Stuart   If this is the alternative, I'd rather be middle-aged. Officially or unofficially.

Oliver   Ah, marketing! Always my Achilles heel. Very well, Stuart can be our lead-off man if he wishes, pattering round the first bend bearing the baton of truth. Don't drop it, Stu-baby! And don't run out of your lane. You wouldn't want to get the lot of us disqualified. Not this early.

I don't care if he goes first. I merely have one request, made on grounds not of egomania, self-interest or marketing, but of decorum, art and a general horror of the banal. Please don't call this next bit 'The Story So Far'. Please don't. Please. Pretty please?

2 : The Story So Far

Stuart   I'm not sure I'm going to be very good at this. I might get things in the wrong order. You're going to have to bear with me. But I think it's best you hear my story first.

Oliver and I were at school together. We were best friends. Then I worked for a clearing bank. He was teaching English as a foreign language. Gillian and I met. She was a picture restorer. Well, she still is. We met, we fell in love, we married. I made the mistake of thinking that was the end of the story, when it was only the beginning. I suppose it's a mistake lots of people make. We've seen too many films, read too many books, believed our parents too much. All this was about ten years ago, when we were in our early thirties. Now we're . . . no, I can see you can work that out for yourself.

Oliver stole her off me. He wanted my life so he took it. He made Gill fall in love with him. How? I don't want to know. I don't think I ever want to know that. For a time, when I suspected something was up, I was obsessed with whether or not they were fucking. I asked you to tell me: remember? I pleaded with you: they are fucking, aren't they? I remember asking. You never answered, and I'm grateful for that now.

I did go a bit crazy at the time. Well, that's quite reasonable, quite understandable, isn't it? I head-butted Oliver and practically broke his nose. And when they got married I gatecrashed the reception and made a bit of a scene. Then I went away to the States. I got myself transferred by the firm. To Washington. Funnily enough, the person I stayed in touch with was Mme Wyatt. That's Gillian's mum. She was the only person on my side. We used to correspond.

After a while I went to see them in France. Or rather, I saw them but they didn't see me. They had this stand-up fight in the middle of the village, Oliver hitting her across the face with everyone pretending not to be looking out of their windows. Me included. I was in a little hotel opposite.

Then I went back to the States. I don't know what I'd expected to find when I went to see them – I don't know what I did find – but it didn't help. Did it make matters worse? It certainly didn't make them any better. I think it was the baby that did me in. Without the baby I might have got something out of it.

I don't remember if I told you at the time, but after my marriage broke up I started paying for sex. I'm not ashamed of it particularly. Other people should be ashamed for treating me the way they did. Prostitutes call their work 'business'. 'Doing business?' the query used to go. I don't know if they still say that. I'm out of that world now.

But my point is this. I used to do business for work and then do business for pleasure. And I knew those two worlds pretty well. People who don't know either of them think it's all dog eat dog. That the man in the grey suit is out to chisel you, and that the tart with too much scent will turn out to be a Brazilian transsexual as soon as you lay down your credit card. Well, I can tell you this. Mostly, you get what you pay for. Mostly, people do what they say they will. Mostly, a deal's a deal. Mostly, you can trust people. I don't mean you leave your wallet open on the table. I don't mean you hand out blank cheques and turn your back at the wrong moment. But you know where you are. Mostly.

No, real betrayal occurs among friends, among those you love. Friendship and love are meant to make people behave better, aren't they? But that's not been my experience. Trust leads to betrayal. You could even say that trust invites betrayal. That's what I saw, what I learnt, then. That's my story so far.

Oliver I was dozing, I confess. *Et tu?* O narcoleptic and steatopygous Stuart, he of the crepuscular understanding and the *Weltanschauung* built of Lego. Look, can we please take the longer view? Chou-en-lai, my hero. Or Zhou-en-lai, as he later became. What do you consider to have been the effect on world history of the French Revolution? To which the wise man replied, 'It is too early to tell.'

Or if not quite so Olympian or Confucian a view, then at least let's have some perspective, some shading, some audacious juxtapositions of pigment, OK? Do we not, each of us, write the novel of our life as we go along? But how few, alas, are publishable. Behold the towering slush pile! Don't call us, we'll call you – no, on second thoughts, we won't call you either.

Now, don't rush to judgement on Oliver – I've cautioned you about that before. Oliver is not a snob. At least, not in the straightforward sense. It is not the subject-matter of these novels, or the social location of their protagonists, that is the problem. 'The story of a louse may be as fine as the history of Alexander the Great – everything depends upon the execution.' An adamantine formula, don't you agree? What is needed is a sense of form, control, discrimination, selection, omission, arrangement, emphasis ... that dirty, three-letter word, art. The story of our life is never an autobiography, always a novel – that's the first mistake people make. Our memories are just another artifice: go on, admit it. And the second mistake is to assume that a plodding commemoration of previously fêted detail, enlivening though it might be in a taproom, constitutes a narrative likely to entice the at times necessarily hard-hearted reader. On whose lips rightly lies the perpetual question: why are you telling me this? If for authorial therapy, then don't expect the reader to pick up the psychiatrist's bill. Which is a polite way of saying that the novel of Stuart's life is, frankly, unpublishable. I gave it the first-chapter test, which is normally enough. Sometimes I'll snigger at the last page as well, just to confirm, but in the present instance I simply couldn't face it. Don't think me harsh. Or if you do, acknowledge me harsh but true.

To the point. Every love story begins with a crime. Agreed? How many *grandes passions* kindle between hearts innocent and unentangled elsewhere? Only in medieval romance or the kiddiwink imagination. But among grown-ups? And as Stuart the pocket cyclopaedia chose to remind you, we were all in our early thirties at the time. Everyone has someone, or a piece of someone, or the expectation of someone, or the memory of someone, which or whom they then discard or betray once they meet Mr, Miss, Ms or in the present case Mrs Right. Am I not speaking true? Of course we Tippex out our treachery, purge our perfidy, and offer retrospectively a tabula rasa of the heart on which the great love story is then indicted; but that's all bollocks, isn't it?

And if we are all therefore criminals, which of us shall condemn the other? Is my case more egregious than yours? I was entangled, at the time I met Gillian, with a señorita from the land of Lope, name of Rosa. Unsatisfactorily entangled, but I would say that, wouldn't I? Stuart was doubtless entangled with a ballet class of fantasies and a wank mag of regrets at the time he met Gillian. And Gillian was unequivocally, indeed legally, entangled with the said Stuart at the time she and I met. You will say it is all a matter of degree, and I will reply: no, it is a matter of absolutes.

And if, in your pressingly legalistic way, you insist on bringing charges, then what can I say except *mea culpa, mea culpa, mea culpa*, but I didn't exactly nerve-gas the Kurds, did I? Additionally and alternatively, as the lawyers amongst you bifurcatingly put it, I would argue that the replacement of Stuart by Oliver in the heart of Gillian was – as you silky, wiggy, mouthy bipeds tend not to put it – no bad thing. She was, as the phrase goes, trading up.

Anyway, that was all years ago, a quarter of our lifetimes ago. Doesn't the term *fait accompli* spring to mind? (I shan't push my luck with *droit de seigneur* or *jus primae noctis*.) Hasn't anyone heard of the statute of limitations? Seven years for any number of torts and crimes, as I understand it. Isn't there a statute of limitations for wife-stealing?

Gillian   What people want to know, whether they ask it directly or not, is how I fell in love with Stuart and married him, then fell in love with Oliver and married him, all within as short a space as is legally possible. Well, the answer is that I did just that. I don't especially recommend you try it, but I promise it's possible. Emotionally as well as legally.

I genuinely loved Stuart. I fell in love with him straight-forwardly, simply. We got on, the sex worked, I loved the fact that he loved me – and that was it. And then, after we were married, I fell in love with Oliver, not simply at all, but very complicatedly, entirely against my instincts and my reason. I refused it, I resisted it, I felt intensely guilty. I also felt intensely excited, intensely alive, intensely sexy. No, as a matter of fact we didn't 'have an affair', as the saying goes. Just because I'm half French people start muttering *ménage à trois*. It wasn't remotely like that. It felt much more primitive for a start. And besides, Oliver and I didn't sleep with one another until Stuart and I had separated. Why are people such experts on what they don't know about? Everyone 'knows' that it was all about sex, that Stuart wasn't much good in bed, whereas Oliver was terrific, and that while I might look pretty level-headed I'm a flirt and a tart and probably a bitch as well. So if you really want to know, the first time Oliver and I went to bed together he had a serious attack of first-night nerves and absolutely nothing happened. The second night wasn't much better. Then we got going. In a funny sort of a way, he's much more insecure in that area than Stuart.

The point is, you can love two people, one after the other, one interrupting the other, like I did. You can love them in different ways. And it doesn't mean one love is true and the other is false. That's what I wish I could have convinced Stuart. I loved each of them truly. You don't believe me? Well, it doesn't matter, I no longer argue the case. I just say: it didn't happen to you, did it? It happened to me.

And looking back, I'm surprised it doesn't happen more often. Long afterwards my mother said, apropos of some other emotional situation, I can't remember, some twosome or threesome, she said, 'The heart has been made tender, and that is dangerous.' I could see what she meant. Being in love makes you liable to fall in love. Isn't that a terrible paradox? Isn't that a terrible truth?

3 : Where Were We?

Oliver   Where were we? For the moment, a tangential observation. Strange how each of those three words encloses its successor, each shedding of letters echoing the sense of loss we always feel when casting the Orphean glance over the shoulder. A poignant diminution, once noticed. Compare and contrast – as the pedagogues used to put it – the lives of the principal English Romantic poets. Align them first by length of name: Wordsworth, Coleridge, Shelley, Keats. Now consider their respective dates: 1770–1850, 1772–1834, 1792–1822, 1795–1821. What delight for the numerologist and truffler of arcana! The man with the longest name lived the longest, the one with the shortest lived the shortest, and so on in between. Better still, the first-born died the last, the last-born died the first! They tuck into one another like Russian dolls. Enough to make you believe in divine purpose, eh? Or at least, divine coincidence.

Where were we? All right, just this once I'll play the game of plodding particularity. I'll pretend that memory is laid out like a newspaper. Very well: turn to the foreign news, colour stories, very very downpage. Small Incident in Minervois Village: Not Many Killed.

I was just, at that random moment you choose to specify, disappearing from your sight (perhaps for ever, you thought; perhaps you loosed a cry of 'Good riddance' in the general direction of my vulnerable scapulae), taking the corner by the Cave Coopérative in my trusty Peugeot. A 403, you surely recall? Tiny radiator grille like a gaoler's spyhole. Greeny-grey livery redolent of an epoch doubtless due for revival. Don't you find it wearisome that nowadays they revive and fetishise decades almost before they're finished? There should be a reverse statute of limitations. No, you *may not* revive the Sixties: it's still only the Eighties. And so on.

So there I was, two-wheeling out of your sight past glinting steel silos crammed with the crushed blood of the Minervois grape, while Gillian was doing a fast-fade in my rear-view mirror. A gauche term, don't you find – rear-view mirror – so filled with plod and particularity? Compare the snappier French: *rétroviseur*. Retrovision: how much we wish we had it, eh? But we live our lives without such useful little mirrors magnifying the road just travelled. We barrel up the A61 towards Toulouse, looking ahead, looking ahead. Those who forget their history are condemned to repeat it. The *rétroviseur*: essential for not just road safety but the race's survival. Oh dear, I feel an advertising slogan coming on.

Gillian   Where were we? I was standing in the middle of the village street in my dressing-gown. There was blood on my face, and it had dripped onto Sophie. Spots of blood on a baby's forehead: like some Black Sabbath blessing. I looked a fright anyway, which was deliberate. I'd been getting at Oliver for a day or more, nagging at him, working him up to a pitch. It was all planned. All my plan. I knew Stuart would be watching. I made a very specific calculation. I thought that if Stuart could see Oliver being vile to me, and me being vile to Oliver, he'd think our marriage wasn't to be envied and that would help him get on with his own life. My mother told me how he'd visit her and go on for hours about the past. I was trying to break that cycle for him, give him – what's that word people use? – give him closure. My other calculation was that Oliver and I would get through it, that I could manage things. That's what I'm good at, after all.

So I was standing there like a scarecrow, like a mad-woman. The blood was from Oliver hitting me with the car keys in his hand. I knew the village's eyes were on me. I knew we'd have to leave. The French are much more bourgeois than the British when it comes down to it. The proprieties matter. Anyway, I'd tell Oliver that being in the village was part of the trouble.

But of course the eyes which were on me that really counted were Stuart's. I knew he was there, up in his hotel room. And I was thinking: have I got away with it? Will I make it work?

Stuart   Where were we? I remember exactly where I was. The room cost 180 francs a night, and the wardrobe door swung open again every time you shut it. The television had an indoor aerial which you had to keep adjusting. Dinner was trout with almonds followed by *crème caramel*. I slept badly. Breakfast was an extra thirty francs. Before breakfast I would stand at my window, looking across to their house.

That morning I was watching Oliver drive off, doing his car no good, racing the engine in second. He seemed to have forgotten there were another two gears available. He's always been hopeless with machinery. My window was open and I could hear this screeching from the car, and it was as if the whole village was screeching, and my head was screeching too. And there in the middle was Gillian. Still in her dressing-gown, the baby in her arms. She was turned away from me so I couldn't see her face. A couple of cars went past, but it was as if she hadn't heard them. She just stood there like a statue, looking in the direction Oliver had gone. After a while, she turned round and stared more or less straight at me. Not that she could have seen me, or known I was there. She had a handkerchief pressed against her face. Her dressing-gown was bright yellow, which seemed all wrong. Then she went slowly back into the house and shut the door.

I thought: so it's come to this?

Then I went downstairs and had breakfast (30FF).

4: In the Meantime

Gillian　　When we were in France we knew a pair of nice middle-aged Englishmen with a house up in the hills where the *garrigue* starts. One of them was a truly terrible painter and I had to be tactful about that. But they were one of those couples you meet from time to time who seem to have got their lives worked out. They'd cleared the land themselves and left the olive trees; there was a terrace and a small pool, art books and a pile of vine logs for barbecues; they even seemed to know the secret of getting a breeze to blow on a hot day. One of the best things about them was that they never gave us advice – you know, third stallholder on the left in the Tuesday market in the lower town of Carcassonne if you want the best . . . and you can't trust plumbers except for . . . I used to take Sophie up there on

21

hot afternoons. One day we were sitting on the terrace, and Tom looked away from me, down the valley. 'Not that it's any of our business,' he murmured, as if to himself, 'but all I'd say is, never get ill in a foreign language.'

It became a sort of house joke. If Sophie sneezed, Oliver would come over all serious and say, 'Now, Soph, don't get ill in a foreign language.' I can see him now, rolling around on the floor with her like a puppy, talking joined-up nonsense all the time, holding her up to look at the scarlet flowers on his climbing beans. I can't say the last ten years have been easy, but Oliver's always been a good father, whatever else you think of him.

But I realised that Tom meant something more general. He wasn't talking about knowing the French for antibiotics – anyway, my French is good enough, and Oliver always got by, even if it meant spouting opera in the *pharmacie*. No, he meant: if you're going to be an expatriate, make sure you've got the temperament for it because anything that goes wrong gets exaggerated. Everything that goes right makes you feel terrifically pleased with yourself – you made the right decision, you made the break – but anything that goes wrong – quarrels, drains, unemployment, whatever – is likely to be twice as much nuisance.

So I knew that if things were going to be rough for a while, we ought to come home. Apart from not wanting to face the village. So by the time Oliver got back from Toulouse on that fateful day I'd put the house with an estate agent and arranged to leave the keys with Mme Rives. I was very straightforward with Oliver; that's to say, as straightforward as you can be when you're keeping up a major deceit. I told him France wasn't working out. I told him the jobs weren't coming my way. I told him we should be grown-up enough to admit that the experiment had failed. And so on. I blamed myself. I was calm throughout, but said I'd been feeling stress, and admitted my jealousy of that girl he'd been teaching was irrational and unfounded. Finally, I said there was no reason why he shouldn't bring his beloved Peugeot back to England. And that, I think, was the key which turned the lock. Oh, yes, and I'd made a good dinner.

In short, it was one of those scenes common to all marriages, where things are half-talked about, and then a decision is made based on all the other things you haven't talked about.

We came home. Another thing we hadn't talked about was having another child. I thought we needed the cement. So for as long as was necessary I was a little less careful, and Marie came along. Oh, don't look at me like that. Half the marriages I know began with an unexpected pregnancy, and quite a few have had a tricky patch glossed over with another baby. That's probably how you came into the world yourself, if you care to delve into your own history.

I picked up my professional life again. I still had contacts. I took on Ellie as my assistant. We rent a small studio half a mile away. We really need a bigger space, as the work's been expanding. Well, it needed to. I've been the breadwinner most of the time. It's been tough on Oliver. He's got lots of energy but he's not . . . robust.

Life has settled down again. I love my work, I love my children. Oliver and I get on well. I never expected him to be a nine-to-fiver when I married him. I encourage his projects, but I don't necessarily count on them coming to anything. He's companionable, he's funny, he's a good father, he's nice to come home to. He cooks. I take everything on a day-to-day basis. That's the only way, isn't it?

Look, I'm not Little Mary Sunshine. There've been ... bad times. And I'm a normal mother, that's to say in the night I have terrible fears. And in the daytime too. Sophie and Marie have only got to behave like the normal, lively girls they are – they've only got to behave as if they trusted the world, as if the world was going to be nice to them, they've only got to leave the house with that optimism on their faces – for my stomach to get tight with fear.

Stuart Some clichés are true. Like America being the land of opportunity. At least, *a* land of opportunity. Some clichés aren't true, like Americans having no sense of irony, or America being a melting pot, or America being the home of the brave and the land of the free. I lived there for almost ten years and knew lots of Americans and liked them. I even married one of them.

But they're not British. Even the ones who look British aren't British, especially them. Which is fine by me. What's that other cliché? Two nations separated by a common language? Yes, that's true too. When someone used to shout at me, 'How ya doin'?' I'd automatically wave and holler back, 'Good,' though sometimes I'd deliberately put on a very English accent, which made them laugh. I'd say things like 'I guess' and 'Sure' and 'You got it', and probably other stuff I didn't notice.

But it's what's underneath the words that makes the difference. For instance, my marriage – my second one, my American one – ended in divorce after five years. Now in England the voice-over would go, 'His marriage failed after five years.' I mean the voice-over in your own head, the one that comments on your life as you live it. But in the States the voice-over went, 'His marriage succeeded for five years.' They're a nation of serial marriers, the Americans. I'm not referring to the Mormons, either. I think it's because at heart they're a profoundly optimistic people. There may be other explanations, but that's the one I believe.

Anyway, I'd better get on with my story. I was with the bank, in Washington, and after a couple of years, I started to become a bit American. I went native. Not native American, but . . . Anyway. In Britain I'd have been sitting across a desk from people authorising small loans and thinking that in time – if I remained diligent and responsible – I would be in a position to authorise larger loans. But after a year or two in the States, I started to think: why him, why her, why not me? So I crossed to the other side of the desk.

I opened a restaurant with a friend. This may surprise you, and it would have surprised me in England. But not over there. Over there you are a realtor one day and training to be a judge the next. I liked food, I understood money, I had a friend who cooked well. We found a site, got a loan, engaged a designer, hired staff and hey presto – we had a restaurant. Simple. Not simple in the doing, but simple in the thinking, and once you get the thinking right the doing is easier. We called it Le Bon Marché, to suggest reasonable prices as well as fresh produce. The style was fusion – French, Californian, Thai. You'd have liked it.

Then I sold out to my partner and moved down to Baltimore. Started another restaurant. That did well too. But after a while . . . This is the thing about the States. In England it would be called 'not sticking at it' or 'not knowing what you want'. In the States, it's normal. You succeed, you look for something else to succeed at. You fail, you still look for something else to succeed at. Profoundly optimistic, as I say.

Organic food distribution, that's what I got into next. It seemed to me an obvious growth area. You've got an ever-increasing number of consumers, especially in the cities, most of them affluent enough and concerned enough to pay more for uncontaminated produce. And you've got a growing number of producers, naturally in rural areas, many of them too local or too idealistic or too busy to understand distribution. It's a question of making the connection. Farmers' markets are all very well, but in my view they're a promotional thing, almost a tourist thing. Basically, it's a choice between retail outlets and box schemes. The box schemes are a bit amateurish and the stores often don't know enough about marketing. Or they think that because they're pure and virtuous they don't need to promote themselves. They don't understand that even today – especially today – virtue needs to be marketed.

So that's what I did. Distribution and marketing, that's what I concentrated on. The fact of the matter is, a lot of organic food producers are about as in touch with modern civilisation as the Amish. And a lot of the retail outlets are still run by hippie types who think that being prompt and efficient is disgustingly middle-class and being able to add up correctly is a sin. Whereas their customers are increasingly normal middle-class people who don't particularly need a dose of counter-culture every time they want a parsnip without poison in it. As I say, it was a question of making the connection.

Look, I can see you want me to get on with it. It's just that I happen to feel strongly . . . OK, I can take a hint. So, I did this in Baltimore for a few years, and then I came over to England for a couple of weeks' holiday. And to tell the truth I'm not very good at holidays, and I started looking at local outlets and delivery systems and, frankly, I was a bit shocked. So I decided to come home and set up here. That's what I did in the meantime.

Oliver   In the meantime, the meantime, the only Greenwich meantime . . .

The meantime. Time is mean, that's true. A tricky little soubrette, Time. Drags her feet and pouts her lower lip most of your life, and then just for that brief happy hour, that margarita moment when pleasure seems to be on the house, she zooms past like a waitress on rollerblades. Take the happy hour which began the instant I bent the knee in homage and troth to *ma belle*. How could I know it would end at approximately the moment you and I last parted company? And how to predict when the scowling minx with tray aloft would call happy hour once again? Things were a tad flat and polder-like for a while after our return to

England, I do confess. Then came the annunciation of Marie. She's a little Singapore Sling if ever there was one.

And there's been more than the occasional frolic at the funfair, wallow at the waterhole, since then. The death of my father, that was a real corners-up day. Some toilsome cyclopaedists of the psyche, earnest calibrators of angst, have apparently estimated that the stress resulting from death of the father is right up there with the pain of moving house. They may have put it the other way round, but even so. In my case, I was much more worried about losing the stair carpet and the Donald Duck lampshade than the paterfamilias.

Oh, don't make that face. You never knew my father, did you? And in the unlikely event that you did, he was never *your* father, he was only ever mine, the Old Bastard. Used to beat me up with a hockey stick when I was barely weaned. Or was it a billiard cue? All because I looked like my mother. All because she died when I was six and he couldn't bear the resemblance. Oh, there were spurious pretexts: my studied insolence – my impromptu insolence as well – plus a certain juvenile zeal on my part for arson, but I knew what it was about. He was a cold fish, my father. The old halibut smoked a pipe to conceal the piscine odours. And then, one day, his scales dried out and his fins turned stiff as a cast-off paintbrush. He had expressed a yen for cremation, but I had him buried at the crossroads with a stake through his heart, just to make sure.

He left what is mockingly known as his estate – more an allotment – we are talking picayunes here, not gold moidores – in trust for Sophie and Marie. With the specific instruction that the said N. Oliver Russell should not be allowed to get his phalanges anywhere near the moolah. Also left letters addressed to the said granddaughters explaining why. The envelopes were, shall we say, lightly gummed. Inside was a mixture of magical realism and hard-core libel. For the children's sake, I cast them into some convenient *oubliette*. My wife disgraced me by crying at the funeral. There had obviously been a three-line whip at the Old Folkery where Monsieur Halibut passed his sunset years, and the tiny flint-'n'-brick tabernacle was full of replacement hips and dental implants belting out their belief in the resurrection of the body, a concept alarming enough at the best of times, but transcendently poo-scary in the present instance. Doubtless Gillian found it all strangely poignant in a left-field, time-of-the-month kind of way. So she blubbed, despite the firm restraining hand I laid on her. Then it was back to the Old Folkery to hear tales of Papa's derring-do with zimmer frame and colostomy bag. I speak in a general sort of way, as is often the case.

Have I drifted a little from my narrative? Well, such are the privileges of the oral tradition. Don't snap at me, *please*, I'm much more sensitive nowadays. So. Let me try to tabulate my last decennium *à la façon de* Stu. We left France. Gill took us out there; Gill brought us home. What did I say about every marriage containing one moderate and one militant? Our little village house of custard stone was sold to a nickel-fucking Belgian. Alas, not one of the Famous Six. And you know the next bit. Cue Stuart, the man from the life insurance ad on the telly: Once You Get Out of the Property Market, it's Very Hard to Get Back In.

You never said a truer word, Stu-baby. An idyllic sun-warmed Languedoc hideaway with mature vegetable garden buys fifty per cent of a chimney stack in a London postal district whose digits I blush to mention. Even the postman gets lost coming out here. Occasionally you might see a bus, if some disgruntled local manages to hijack one at gunpoint and make it perform a useful social service.

Our union has been blessed with further offspring. Marie, sister to Sophie. How the little ones love their dear papa. They cling to me like a wet shower curtain. Sophie is the serious one, wants everything to be perfect. Marie shows signs of being a proper little madam.

Have I used it before? The line about the shower curtain? You're rather giving me the eye. It's the price of being an entertainer. You scatter your *bons mots* like *bonbons* and every so often someone in the front stalls throws a sweetpaper back. Hey, you, we've had this flavour before. Listen, there aren't that many types of jellybean in the world. You'll be complaining next that all the stories ever written are merely variants on a set prime number of plots. Well, I should know about that, given the screenplay I currently have in development. In development in my head, that is. I confess that some of my artistic ventures over the last decade have had rather *triste* dénouements. I have on occasion been driven back, like a dog returning to its vomit, to Mr Tim's College of English, all to earn the odd drachma and put a stuffed vine leaf on the family table. I fear the spirit of nine-to-five was never very resilient in Oliver.

But across the land it flourishes like the green bay tree. Is it just that I notice these things more? In the years since we returned to Londinium Vetus from the Land which knoweth not the Brussels Sprout, it has increasingly struck me that the disparity between success and failure has never been more – can we escape the word for once? I think not – vulgar. On the one hand, the lustrous off-road vehicles, the Chargers and Thrusters and Cruisers and general Super-turbo Bullybags. And on the other, the frail pizza-delivery lads on frankly underpowered motor scooters, shame-facedly rearranging their customers' toppings as they hurdle a speed bump. Do the pushy power-steerers high above the traffic give a thought to the puttering purveyors of Four Seasons with Extra Onion, hold the Tomato, not the tomato paste just the fresh tomato, and extra peperoni and extra peas as well? Do they give a toss? If hypocrisy is the tribute vice offers to virtue, then style used to be the tribute rich offered to poor. Not any more.

And another thing. If they're called off-road vehicles, why are so many of them *on the fucking road*? Answer me that if you can.

Did you read about those snowfalls in the American Midwest last winter? The snow was as high as an elephant's eye (that's one for you, Stuart). The farmers knew what to do, being, well, farmers, and only left their instant igloos with old-fashioned tennis rackets strapped to their boots. The humble blue-collar worker knew to stay home, fire up the microwave and rewind his Superbowl Highlights tape. Whereas those who were truly fucked were the bourgeois cavaliers in their off-road vehicles, eager for the chance to show all those low-lifes and under-achievers and dullards and rubes and faggots out there how splendid and enviable it is to prance wherever thou wist across the snow crust in four-wheel comfort. But just to prove that there is some sub- or super-lunary justice in this world, they all, every one of them, got stuck up to their relevant pistons or turbines, and had to be dug out by huskies and Mounties.

Do you think there is? Justice in this world, I mean? Do you think virtue is rewarded, vice punished? Do you take the view that virtue is its own reward? Always a rather masturbatory implication to that, I feel. Presumably virtue must learn to be self-pleasuring because nobody else is going to diddle it. Is the same true of its opposite – that vice is its own reward? That sounds closer to the mark. The voluptuary would not indulge if the rewards of *volupté* were not what drew him. Whereas those who comfort the leprous, rend their longjohns into bandages, and generally turn up like a St Bernard on a snowmobile to succour the frost-bitten off-roader – do they get a buzz from the moment of rescue? Is that what the proverb means: that the Lord isn't going to tip them a food stamp for their labours, so they might as well seize what *volupté* they can?

I'm merely a binoculared student of the passing caravan-serai of life. You might find my conclusions rather DIY. But I can't help thinking that most of the time vice gets away with it.

You want a second opinion? I don't blame you. Try this then, from an old Toulousain heretic: 'God is perfect; nothing in the world is perfect; therefore nothing in the world was made by God.' Not bad, eh?

5 : Now

Terri   Mind if I join you? I mean, is this a private thing or what? I could e-mail if you prefer. But I'll tell you one thing, I'm not having five years of my life tossed in the trash like that. I'm not going to be anyone's damn footnote.

When Stuart hired me as maitresse D, he got a good deal and he knew it. A chef may be great or a chef may be shit, but without front-of-house he's got no chance. That's where a restaurant starts. On the phone, at the desk, at the coat-check, in the bar. Skills required: keeping a client happy when he arrives on time and his table isn't ready; dealing with the booking for two that turns up as six; hurrying a table along without letting it know it's being hurried. Little things, big things. Not letting it show on your face when the guy who was so deeply married eight-thirty every Friday starts bringing in his girlfriend on Tuesdays as well. Knowing when a woman asks for the check if it's because she's paying or because she's bored out of her skull. Neutral placement of the check if you aren't sure. Little things, big things.

I was good at all that, so people thought our chef was great even if he was only fair. And when Stuart started sourcing the best organic produce, that could have made him definitely great, except it really pissed him off, because chefs prefer their own suppliers for reasons they keep to themselves. Like, sauces aren't the only things they need to skim, if you follow me.

So we got ourselves a new chef, a better one to start with, except he got pissed off too because he said Stuart didn't know how to buy fish. Meat, vegetables, fruit, OK, but fish, no way. So I was like the UN between the kitchen and the office on top of the front desk. Which, to give Stuart his due, he appreciated.

We have our picture of Brits, especially in a city like Baltimore, which is a very American city in case you never heard. Wallis Simpson came from Baltimore, the one who married your King. We don't get too many of you coming through, so we buy into the stereotype, which is that Brits are snobby and stick together and don't pick up the tab for drinks if they can possibly avoid it. Oh, and most of the men are tea-bags, if you'll pardon the expression. But Stuart wasn't like that. He was a little reserved at first, but he paid full market wages and actually seemed to like Americans. When he asked me for a date I said no, just like that, because I never date in the workplace, never have. Then he came on all Masterpiece Theatre if you know what I mean, about not understanding American etiquette, and respecting me saying no, but might there not, under our mysterious social code, be something in the ballpark between a working relationship and a full date, to which I might, without compromize, feel able to agree. I said: well you can buy me a drink if that's what's on your mind. And we both just laughed.

We took it from there. Look, I'm not going to give you the full picture. Not unless you get down on your knees and beg. But I'd like to say something, before you get in any deeper. Stuart's account of his life probably goes like this: slow out of the blocks, bad first marriage, comes to the States, goes into business, makes a success of it, has a good enough second marriage, it doesn't go the distance, then an amicable divorce, he gets nostalgic for England and decides to apply his business skills back home. Another American success story, don't we just love 'em. Man screws up his life, gets focussed, moves on.

Well, everyone's entitled to their own life story, sure; that's another American freedom. Believe it if you want. Believe it for now.

Stuart   My key words are transparency, efficiency, virtue, convenience and flexibility. Basically, the market divides three ways. Number one, mail order direct from the producers – this works best for meat and poultry – so you know exactly where it comes from. That's transparency. Number two, the supermarkets, who came into the game a bit late, but know how to display and sell, and how to source. That's efficiency. Number three, the local outlets, which are often higgledy-piggledy, like thrift shops, with sacks of filthy recycled plastic bags and dopey staff who really like to finish their conversations with one another before they do anything as humiliatingly businesslike as actually sell you some leeks. That's virtue. Now the modern organic consumer, in my book, is entitled to the best of all three worlds: knowing where the produce comes from, being treated like a proper customer, knowing that what they are doing is right and being prepared to pay a little extra for it. Add in convenience and flexibility and you're there. So I did my research and signed up a few key exclusivities. Eggs, bread, milk, cheese, honey, fruit and veg: those are the bedrock. Fish, no; meat, yes. A few people might be put off by the sight of meat, but I'm not after hard-liners and idealists. I'm after the traditional customer with enough discretionary income and good sense to go organic, who also appreciates one-stop shopping. I don't bother with peripherals like organic wine and beer. I don't try and turn the place into a teashop. Forget the milkchurns of bean soup. Lose those amateurish handwritten signs full of exclamation marks. Hire staff who know how to answer questions and are keen to bag. Tall, brown-paper bags double-folded at the top. Home deliveries. On-line ordering. Special meet-the-supplier events. A monthly newsletter.

You might think that's all pretty obvious. But I never claimed to be a blindingly original thinker. On the whole, blindingly original thinkers go bust. And as I said, some clichés are true. I just looked at the market, worked out what people wanted, did my research and then my sums. I call my shops The Green Grocer. Do you like it? I'm rather proud of it myself. I've got four outlets at the moment, with another two opening next year. I get recommendations on the food pages and in the colour magazines. Someone on the local paper wanted to do a profile of me the other month but I turned it down. I didn't want the news to get out that way. I wanted to wait until the time was right, when I was settled. Which is now.

Gillian   When I said it's been tough on Oliver, I meant it. I'm the one who has the job, who gets out of the house, who meets new people. Oliver's the one still waiting for things to happen.

There was this suggestion in the papers recently that marriage should be treated as a business. Romance never lasts, they said, so couples should negotiate the terms of their partnership in advance: all the conditions and clauses, rights and duties. Actually, it doesn't sound to me like a new idea at all. It reminds me of those old Dutch paintings – husband and wife side by side, gazing out at the world a little complacently, the wife sometimes holding the purse. Marriage as business: look at our profits. Well, I absolutely don't agree. What's the point if the romance isn't still there? What would be the point if I didn't want to come back to Oliver every evening?

Of course we talk about arrangements a lot. That's like any normal marriage. Children, shopping, meals, pick-up times, homework, television, the school run, money, holidays. Then we fall into bed and don't have sex.

Sorry, that's one of Oliver's jokes. At the end of a long day, when work's been a problem and the girls have been a handful, he'll say, 'Let's just fall into bed and not have sex.'

My father – he was a teacher – ran off with one of his pupils when I was thirteen. You knew that, didn't you? Maman never refers to it, or to him – won't even mention his name. I sometimes think, what if he hadn't? What if he'd nearly gone, then changed his mind – decided that marriage was a business – and stayed? Think how many lives would have been completely different. Would I be here now?

I was reading a book the other day – by a woman – and at some point she said something like – I haven't got it here so I can't quote it exactly – something like every relationship contains within it the ghosts, or the shadows, of all the other relationships it isn't. All the abandoned alternatives, the forgotten choices, the lives you could have led but didn't and haven't. I found this thought enormously consoling because it was true, and at the same time enormously upsetting. Do you think that's just a part of growing up, or growing older, whatever we like to call it? I suddenly felt terribly relieved that I'd never had an abortion. I mean, it's lucky – I didn't have anything against it in principle when I was younger. But imagine thinking about that in later life. What never happened. The abandoned alternatives, the unled lives. It's bad enough thinking about it in the abstract. Imagine what it would be like if it was that real.

This is what my life is like now.

Mme Wyatt   'Marriage comes after love as smoke comes after fire.' You remember? Chamfort. Was he saying only that marriage is the inescapable consequence of love, that we cannot have one without the other? A piece of wisdom that is not worth writing down, no? So he is inviting us to look at the comparison more exactly. He is saying, perhaps, that love is dramatic and hot and burning and noisy, while marriage is like a warm fog which stings your eyes and makes it impossible for you to see. He is saying perhaps also that marriage is something blown about by the wind – that love is fierce and burns the ground it stands on, while marriage is a more incoherent condition which can be altered and dissipated by the lightest breeze.

I think this, also, about the comparison. People suppose that when they light a match, the hottest part of it is in the centre of the flame. This is a mistake. The hottest part of the flame is not inside it, but outside it, just above it, in fact. The hottest place is where the fire ends and the smoke begins, exactly there. Interesting, *hein*?

I am considered wise by some people, and that is because I hide my pessimism from them. People want to believe that, yes, things may be bad, but there are always various possible solutions, and when one of them is the case, then things will be better. Patience and virtue and a certain modest heroism will be rewarded. I do not say so, of course, but something in my style implies that all of this is quite possible. Oliver, who pretends, who promises that he is writing films, once told me the old wisdom about Hollywood, that what America seeks is a tragedy with a happy ending. Therefore my advice is also Hollywood, and people

39

think me wise. So, to get a reputation for wisdom you must be a pessimist who predicts a happy ending. But my advice to myself is not Hollywood, it is more classical. I do not believe in the gods, of course, except as a sort of metaphor. But I do believe that life is tragic, if it is possible to use that term still. Life is a process during which your weakest places are inevitably discovered. It is also a process during which you are punished for your earlier actions and desires. Not punished justly, oh no – that is part of what I mean by not believing in the gods – simply punished like that. Punished anarchically, if you like.

I do not think that I will have another lover in my lifetime. That is a thing you have to acknowledge at a certain point. No, no, do not flatter me. Yes, I look a few years younger than I am, but that is no particular compliment to a Frenchwoman who has spent as much money on *produits de beauté* as I have during the years. It is not the case that it is no longer possible. These things are always possible, and in these matters one can always pay, officially or unofficially – oh, stop looking shocked – but it is more that I do not want to. Ah, Mme Wyatt, you cannot say that, you never know when love will not strike, it is always the dangerous time as you once told us, and so on. You misunderstand me. It is not so much that I do not want, as that I do not want to want. I do not desire to desire. And I will say this: I am perhaps now as happy as in the years when I did desire. I am less occupied, less preoccupied, but no less happy. Or no less unhappy. Is this perhaps my punishment from those gods who no longer exist – to realise that all the heart trouble – is that the word? – which I endured, all that searching and all that pain, all that expectation, all those actions, were not, after all, as I thought, relevant to happiness? Is this my punishment?

Such is how things are for me now.

Ellie   Took me a long time before I could call her Gillian. Did it on the phone first, tried it out talking to other people about her, finally did it to her face. She's that sort of person, very together, very sure of herself. And she's nearly twice as old as me anyway. I mean, I'm assuming she's in her early forties. Wouldn't dream of asking her. Though if I did, I bet she'd tell me straight out.

You should hear her on the phone. I wouldn't dare say some of the things she says. I mean, they're the truth, but that makes it worse, doesn't it? You see, there are clients who send us work because they secretly hope we'll find Leonardo's signature underneath all the crud and make them pots of money. Yes, it is often as simple as that. They haven't got any evidence, they've just got this belief, and they somehow think that sending the picture off for cleaning and analysis will prove their hunch was correct. That's what they're paying us for, right? And most of the time we know just by looking, but because Gillian likes to work with all the evidence, she doesn't tell them what they're hoping is out of the question, and because she hasn't actually said it, that raises their expectations even higher. And then in the end, ninety-nine times out of a hundred, she has to tell them. And some of them take it like a poke in the eye.

'No, I'm afraid not,' she'll go.

Then there'll be a long blast down the other end of the phone.

'I'm afraid that's just not possible.'

More blast.

'Yes, it could be a copy of a painting that's been lost, but even so we're talking about 1750, 1760 at the very earliest.'

Short blast.

Gillian: 'Well, let's call it cadmium yellow if you wish, though cadmium wasn't discovered until 1817. Yellow of this mixture did not exist before 1750.'

Short blast.

'Yes, I am "only" a restorer. That's to say, I can date a painting within certain parameters from analysis of the pigment. There are other ways to date pictures. For instance, if you're an amateur, you can have "a certain feel" for pictures, and then really you can date them whenever you like.'

This normally shuts them up, not surprisingly. But not always.

'No, we removed the overpainting.'

'No, we analysed all the paint layers back to the canvas.'

'No, you agreed to that.'

'No, we haven't "damaged" it.'

She keeps her cool, all the way through. Then she says, 'I've got one suggestion.' Then she pauses to make sure she's got the man's attention. 'When you've paid our bill and when you've collected the painting, we'll send you our full pigment analysis and report, and if you don't like it you can burn it.'

That usually ends the conversation. And Gillian, when

42

she puts down the phone, looks – what? – not exactly triumphant, but sure of herself.

'He won't be back in a hurry,' I say, meaning partly: aren't you turning away business?

'I won't work for pigs like that,' she says.

You might think this was just a quiet, scientific job, but there can be a lot of pressure put on you. This man, he'd spotted a painting in a provincial auction, his wife liked it, and because it was very dark and a biblical scene, he decided it was by Rembrandt. Or if not, then by 'someone like Rembrandt', as he put it, as if there was any such person. He'd paid £6,000 for it, and he clearly regarded the cleaning and analysis as an investment to make that initial outlay grow into tens or hundreds of thousands. He didn't like being told that what he had at the end of it was a cleaner picture, properly restored, still worth about £6,000, as long as someone else wanted to pay that much for it.

She's very straight, Gillian. And she's got a very good eye for fakes. Human as well as artistic. Then and now.

Oliver Now here's a funny thing. I dropped my little testamentary heirs and assigns off at the local force-feeding establishment, where the pretty little goslings have their throats gently massaged while the Big Honker pours in knowledge like so much corn. The flat looked as if the *lares et penates* had done some heavy partying, and my artistic yen to reduce chaos to order being what it is, I'd stacked a few things in the sink, and was just trying to decide whether to give the Unpublished Shorter Fiction of Saltykov-Shche-drin another go or have a three-hour wank (don't be envious, only teasing), when the shrill borborygmus of the telephone alerted me to what philosophers preposterously maintain is the outside world. Might it be some Hollywood exec, propelled by the unputdownability of my screenplay into unfamiliar nocturnal existence: the slow loris of Malibu, the Edward's potto of Bel Air? Or might it, more plausibly, be some drubbingly mercantile reminder from my dear *moglie* about the projected shortage in the short to medium term of washing-up liquid? But reality proved – and in this respect the philosophers have down the millennia been altogether too dismayingly right – not entirely as I imagined.

'Hello, it's Stewart,' said a rather smug voice.

'Well, good for you,' I replied with all the acerbity of matutinal melancholy. (They're always far worse in the morning, the glooms, don't you find? As far as I have a theory on the matter, it goes like this. The layout of the day, such as it ineluctably is – dawn, morning, afternoon, dusk, night – represents such a bloody obvious paradigm of the transit of human existence, that while the approach of felty dusk, with obliterating night on its coat-tails, is a forgivable time to suffer a heightened awareness of human frangibility and inevitable fucking demise, and while early afternoon is a similarly logical location, as the echo of the midday gun wails like tinnitus in your ear, the notion of cornflake *tristesse*, of yoghurt despair, is prima facie contradictory, if not an insult to the metaphor. Which contradiction makes the black dog's teeth the sharper in the morning, irony bubbling like rabies in its saliva.)

'Oliver,' the voice repeated, manifestly cowed by my rebuke. 'It's Stuart.'

'Stuart,' I replied, and immediately felt I had to play for time. 'Sorry, I heard you as a Stewart.'

He didn't respond to this. 'So how are things?' he asked.

'Things', I replied, 'are, depending upon your philosophy, either a great illusion or really and truly the only "things" there are.'

'Same old Oliver,' he chuckled admiringly.

'Now *that*', I riposted, 'is a matter for physiological as well as philosophical debate.' I gave him some top-of-the-head summary of cell replacement strategy, and the likely percentage of Oliver-tissue still present from the artefact he had last glimpsed however many millennia previously.

'I thought we could meet.'

It was only then that I realised he was not some phantasmagorical emanation of my morning mood, or even – briefly acknowledging the 'world' to be such as many perceive it – calling long distance. Stu-baby – my Stu-baby – was back in town.

6 : Just Stuart

Stuart   Oliver seemed rather taken aback to hear from me. Well, I suppose that's not surprising. The person making the phone call is always thinking more about the recipient of the call than vice versa. There are people who ring up and say, 'Hi, it's me,' as if there was only one person in the world called Me. Though, in a funny way, while this is a bit irritating, you usually do guess who's at the other end, so in a way there is only one Me.

Sorry, that's a bit off the point.

After he'd got over his initial shock, Oliver asked, 'How did you track us down?'

I thought about this for a moment, then said, 'I looked you up in the phone book.'

Something about the way I said it made Oliver get the

giggles, just like he did in the old days. It was a sound from the past, and after a while I joined in, even if I didn't find it as funny as he obviously did.

'Same old Stuart,' he finally said.

'Up to a point,' I replied, meaning: don't jump to conclusions.

'How so not?' – which is a typical Oliver way of phrasing the question.

'Well, the hair's gone grey for a start.'

'Really? Who was it used to maintain that prematurely grey hair was the sign of a charlatan? One of the wits and dandies.' He started listing names, but I didn't have all day.

'I've been accused of many things, but being a charlatan won't hold water.'

'Oh, Stuart, I didn't mean *you*,' he said, and I even sort of believed him. 'With you such an accusation would be a veritable colander. You could drain pasta in such a charge. You could –'

'How about Thursday? I'm out of town until then.'

He consulted a non-existent diary – I can always tell when people do that – and managed to fit me in.

Gillian   After you've lived with someone for a while, you can always tell when they're holding something back, can't you? The same way you can tell if they're not listening, or would rather not be in the same room as you, or . . . all those other things.

I've always found it touching, the way Oliver stores up things to tell me, then comes like a child with both hands cupped together. I suppose it's partly his nature, partly the fact that not enough happens to him. One thing I know about Oliver is that he'd be really good at being a success, he'd enjoy it to the maximum, and in a funny sort of way it wouldn't spoil him. I really believe that.

We were having our supper. Pasta, with a tomatoey sauce Oliver had made. 'Twenty questions,' he said, just at the moment I thought he would. We've taken to playing this game, not least because it spins out delivery of the news. I mean, I don't have that much to tell Oliver either, after a day in the studio, half-listening to the radio and half-chatting to Ellie. Boyfriend problems, most of the time.

'All right,' I said.

'Guess who phoned?'

And without thinking, I replied, 'Stuart.'

Without thinking, as I said. Without thinking that I was spoiling Oliver's game, apart from anything else. He looked at me as if I'd been cheating, or tipped off in some way. He obviously couldn't believe that it had come to me just like that.

There was a silence, then Oliver said, in a really petulant voice, 'What colour's his hair then?'

'What colour's Stuart's hair?' I repeated, as if this were a normal kind of conversation we were having. 'Well, it's a sort of mousey-brown.'

'Wrong!' he shouted. 'He's gone grey! Who said it was the sign of a charlatan? Not Oscar. Beerbohm? His brother? Huysmans? Old Joris-Karl – ?'

'You've seen him?'

'No,' he replied, sounding not exactly triumphant, but at

least as if he was in charge again. I let it go – I mean, the part to do with marital challenge.

Oliver filled me in. Apparently, Stuart is married to an American woman, he's become a greengrocer, and his hair has gone grey. I say apparently because Oliver's apt to be a bit approximate in the news-gathering business. He also didn't seem to have found out various key things, like how long Stuart is over for, and why, and where he's staying.

'Twenty questions,' said Oliver for the second time. He was a bit more relaxed by now.

'All right.'

'What herb, spice or other wholesome additive, nutrient or condiment did I put in the sauce?'

I didn't get it in twenty. Perhaps I wasn't trying very hard.

Later, I thought: how did I guess Stuart straight away? And why did it give me a jolt when I heard he was married? No, it wasn't as simple as that. 'Married' is one thing, and no surprise with someone you haven't seen for ten years. No, it was 'married to an American woman' that gave me the jolt. That's pretty vague; but suddenly, just for a moment, it all seemed a bit too specific.

'Why now?' I asked on the Thursday, when Oliver was setting off for his drink with Stuart.

'What do you mean, why now? It's six. I've got to be there at six-thirty.'

'No, why now? Why is Stuart getting in touch with us now? After all this time. Ten years.'

'I expect he wants to make up.' I must have looked at him in disbelief. 'You know, as in, be forgiven.'

'Oliver, *we* did *him* damage, not the other way round.'

'Oh well,' said Oliver cheerfully, 'it's all blood under the bridge by now.' Then he squawked and waggled his elbows like a chicken, which is his way of saying 'must fly'. I once pointed out to him that chickens didn't fly, but he said that was part of the joke.

Stuart   I'm not much of a one for the touchy-feely stuff. I mean, a handshake is one thing, and sex is another – at the opposite end of the spectrum, naturally. And there's foreplay, which I also enjoy. But all the shoulder-slapping, body-hugging, bicep-punching, hi-fiving side of human behaviour – which, when you come to think of it, is all human *male* behaviour – sorry, I can't do it. Not that it mattered in the States. They just thought it was where I come from, and I only had to say, 'I'm afraid I'm just a tight-assed limey,' for them to understand and laugh and slap me on the shoulder some more. And that was OK.

Oliver has always been a hand-on-the-wrist type of person. He links arms at the slightest opportunity. He's a two-cheek kisser, and what he really likes to do is take a woman's head in his hands, one paw on either side of her forehead, and then slobber all over her, which I find rather repulsive. It's how he sees himself. As if to prove that he's the relaxed one, he's leading the show.

So I wasn't at all surprised at his reaction when we met again for the first time in ten years. I stood up, extended my hand for him to shake, which he did, but then he kept my hand in his and ran his left hand up my arm. He squeezed my elbow a little, then my shoulder a bit more, then ran his hand up to my neck and gave that a squeeze, and finally sort of ruffled the back of my head as if drawing attention to the fact that I've gone grey. If you saw that sort of greeting in the movies, you'd suspect that Oliver was a mafioso reassuring me that everything was fine while another villain crept up behind me with a garotte.

'What can I get you?' I asked.

'Pint of Skullsplitter, old friend.'

'I'm not sure they have that, you know. They've got Belhaven Wee Heavy. Or what about a Pelforth Amberley?'

'Stuart. *Stu-art*. Joke. Skullsplitter. Joke.'

'Ah,' I said.

He asked the barman what wines they had by the glass, nodded several times, and ordered a large vodka tonic.

'Well, you haven't changed, you old sod,' Oliver told me. No, I haven't: ten years older, hair gone grey, no longer wear specs, lost a stone and a half thanks to my exercise programme, and dressed from head to foot in American clothes. Yup, same old Stuart. Of course, he may have meant internally, but that would have been a bit premature.

'Nor have you.'

'*Non illegitimi carborundum*,' he replied, but it looked to me as if the bastards had ground him down quite a bit. His hair was the same length, and the same black, but his face was a bit lined, and his linen suit – which looked remarkably like the one he had ten years ago – had various stains and marks on it, which in the old days would have seemed bohemian, but now just looked shabby. His shoes were black-and-white patents. Pimp's shoes – except they were all scuffed. So he looked just like Oliver, only more down-at-heel. On the other hand, it might have been me that had changed. Perhaps he'd remained exactly the same; it was just how I was seeing him now.

He filled me in on the last ten years. It all sounds pretty rosy. Gillian's career has really taken off since they came back to London. Their two daughters are a pride and joy. They're living in an up-and-coming part of town. And Oliver himself has 'several projects in development'.

Not so many that he could afford to buy his own round (you'll have to forgive me for noticing such things). He didn't exactly ply me with questions either, though he did ask at one point how my 'greengrocery business' was getting along. I said it was . . . profitable. This wasn't the first word that came to mind, but it was the word I wanted Oliver to hear. I could have said it was fun, or a challenge, or time-consuming, or hard work, or whatever, but the way he asked the question made me pick the word profitable.

He nodded in a slightly resentful way, as if there was some direct connection between people voluntarily handing over money for the best organic produce at The Green Grocer and other people not handing over money to Oliver to help him 'develop his projects'. And as if it was my duty, as the champion of the profit principle, to feel guilty about this. But I don't, you see.

And here's another thing. You know how some friend-ships get stuck the way they were when they first began? Like in families, where someone's still the little sister in the eyes of her big brother even though she's drawing her pension. Well, that's all changed between Oliver and me. I mean, in the pub he still treated me as if I was his kid sister.

52

It's the same for him. But not for me. I feel quite different now.

Afterwards, I ran through some of the questions he didn't ask. In the old days I might have felt a bit hurt. Not any more. I wonder if he noticed that I didn't ask anything about Gillian. I let him tell me, but I didn't ask.

Gillian   Sophie was doing her homework when Oliver came home. He was a bit drunk – not pissed, but in that three-drinks-on-an-empty-stomach mood. You know the scenario – the man returning home and half-expecting praise for doing so? Because in the back of his mind is the time before he got married when the evening would have rolled on without let or hindrance? So there's a little edge of I don't know what, aggression, resentment, which you in turn resent, because after all you didn't stop him going out and you honestly wouldn't mind if he stayed out longer, in fact all evening, because you like an evening alone with the children from time to time. Which makes things a little strained.

'Where've you been, Daddy?'

'Down the pub, Soph.'

'Are you drunk?'

Oliver wheeled around the room, doing drunk and breathing all over Sophie, who pretended to faint and wave the fumes away with her hand.

'Who've you been getting drunk with?'

'An old friend. An old mucker. An American plutocrat.'

'What's a plutocrat?'

'Someone who earns more than I do.' Like the rest of the world, I thought.

'Did he get drunk too?'

'Drunk? He got so drunk his contact lenses fell out.'

Sophie laughed. I relaxed. For a moment. Wrongly. Do you think children have an instinct at such times?

'So who is he?'

Oliver looked at me. 'He's just Stuart.'

'That's a funny name – Just Stuart.'

'Well, he's a lawyer, you see. In all respects except that of actually being a lawyer.'

'Daddy, you *are* drunk.' Oliver breathed over her again, Sophie gagged again, and seemed to be going back to her homework. 'So how do you know him?'

'Him?'

'Just Stuart the Plutocrat.'

Again Oliver looked at me. I couldn't tell if Sophie was picking up on it. 'How do we know Just Stuart?' he asked me. Oh, thanks a bunch, I thought. You keep *your* hands clean. I also thought: now isn't the time.

'He was someone we knew,' I said rather vaguely.

'Obviously,' she replied, sounding older than her years.

'Sandwich,' I said to Oliver. 'Bed,' I said to Sophie. They know that voice of mine. I know it too, and don't like to hear it too often. But what else can you do?

Oliver was away in the kitchen for quite a while and came back with a big chip butty. He's got this deep fryer he's ridiculously proud of, with some kind of filter that's meant to absorb the fumes. It doesn't, of course.

'The secret of a good chip butty,' he said, not for the first time, 'is that the heat of the chips melts the butter on the bread.'

'So?'

'So that it runs down your wrists.'

'No. So – Stuart?'

'Ah, Stuart. He's in the pink. In the grey. In the money. Wouldn't let me buy my round – you know how it is when plutocracy strikes.'

'I don't think either of us knows that.'

According to Oliver, Stuart is the same as ever, apart from being a plutocrat, and a beer bore who talks a lot about pigs.

'Are you seeing him again?'

'Didn't arrange to.'

'Have you got his number?'

Oliver gave me a look and slopped up some butter from his plate. 'He didn't give it me.'

'You mean he refused?'

There was some chewing, then a stagey sigh. 'No, I mean that I didn't at any point ask and he didn't at any point offer.'

I felt relieved when I heard this. It was worth Oliver's irritation. He's probably just over on a brief trip.

Do *I* want to see Stuart again? I asked myself that question later. And I don't know the answer. I'm usually good at making my mind up about things – well, someone has to be around here – but I realise that when it comes to this, I want someone else to make the decision for me.

Anyway, I shouldn't think it will arise.

Terri   I have friends living out on the Bay. They told me how the crabbers work. They start in the middle of the night, around two-thirty, and go through till the morning. They lay out this line, that can be as long as five hundred yards, with weights every few yards and the bait's attached to them. The bait they use is generally eel. Then after they've laid out the line, they begin to pull it in, and this is where you need a good eye and a lot of skill. The crabs will be holding onto the eel, but crabs aren't stupid, they aren't going to let themselves be pulled up into the air and just picked off and flung into the basket, are they? So just before the crab comes to the surface, just before it might let go, the crabber has to reach smoothly into the water and scoop it out.

As my friend Marcelle says: remind you of something?

Stuart   What did you think of Oliver's behaviour? I mean, honestly? I don't know what I was expecting. Perhaps I was expecting something I couldn't admit to myself. But I'll tell you this. I wasn't expecting *nothing*. I wasn't expecting, Hi Stuart, my old chum, my old mucker, haven't seen you for a few years, yes you may buy me a drink, and then another, let me touch my forelock to you kind sir, and another, and in between I'll carry on patronising you just where I left off. That's what I call nothing. Perhaps it was a bit naïve of me.

But there are lots of things about life that aren't straightforward, don't you find? Not liking your friends, for instance. Or rather, liking them and not liking them at the

56

same time. Not that I think of Oliver as a friend any more, of course. Although he obviously still thinks of me as a friend. You see, that's another complication: A thinks of B as a friend, but B doesn't think of A as a friend. Friendship can be more complicated than marriage, if you ask me. I mean, marriage, that's the ultimate challenge for most people, isn't it? The moment when you put your whole life on the line, when you say, here I am, this is what I stand for, I'll give you everything I've got. I don't mean worldly goods, I mean heart and soul. In other words, we're aiming for a hundred per cent, aren't we? Now we may not get that hundred per cent, most likely we won't, or we might get it for a while and then settle for less, but we'll be aware of that figure, that completeness, existing. What used to be called an ideal. I guess we call it a target nowadays. And then when things go wrong, when the percentage drops below an agreed target figure – say fifty per cent – you have this thing called divorce.

But with friendship, it's not so simple, is it? You meet someone, you like them, you do things together – and you're friends. But you don't have a ceremony saying you are, and you don't have a target. And sometimes you're only friends because you have friends in common. And there are friends you don't see for a while who you pick up with straight away, right where you left off; and others where you have to start all over again. And there's no divorce. I mean, you can quarrel, but that's another thing. Now Oliver just thought we could pick up from where we'd left off – no, from a point some way *before* we left off. Whereas I wanted to look and see.

57

What I saw, in a nutshell, was this. I offer him a drink, he asks for a Skullsplitter. I say what about a Belhaven Wee Heavy. He laughs at me for being a pedant and having a sense-of-humour bypass. 'Joke, Stuart. Joke.' The point is: Oliver doesn't know there *is* a beer called Skullsplitter. It's made in the Orkneys and it's got a wonderfully creamy taste. Someone said it was a bit like fruit cake. Raisiny. That's why I suggested a Belhaven instead. But Oliver doesn't know all this, and it doesn't cross his mind that I do. That after ten years I might know one or two things more than I did before.

Oliver   So what do you think my portly chum is worth? With that question, as with so many others, one may take the high road or the low road, and for once you will catch Oliver snapping the Velcro fasteners on his trampoline-soled trainers and joining the democratic thrum. *La rue basse, s'il vous plaît.* We are not discussing the moral avoirdupois of the said individual, but requiring brusquer information. Stuart: is he replete with the long green? While quaffing and quenching with him I did not, out of sheer tact, enquire too subcutaneously about his sojourn in the Land of the Fee, but it did strike me that if the liquidity was sloshing around his calves like a Venetian flood-tide he might – to switch city-states – care to Medici some of the moolah in my direction. There are times when the artist is not ashamed to play his sempiternal role as the recipient of alms. The lien between art and suffering is a gilded cord which can bind a touch tightly. Another day, another dolour.

And I *am* aware that in the world of PC Plod's notebook, the Puginesque witness box, and the gnarled hand on the Bible, in the world of Mr-Valiant-for-Truth, Stuart is not in the strictest sense of the term portly. If anything, his corporeal lineaments suggest the rank axillary fug of the gymnasium, or the spiritual aridity of the domestic exercise bicycle. Perhaps he swings a pair of Indian clubs while yodelling along to his Frank Ifield records. Don't ask *me*. All *I* pump is irony.

I also, you might have noticed, deal in subjective truth – so much more real, and more reliable, than the other sort – and according to that criterion Stuart was, is now, and ever more shall be so, portly. His soul is portly, his principles are portly, and I trust his deposit account is portly too. Do not be misled by the slim husk he currently presents for inspection.

He did tell me one interesting fact, which may or may not relate to the above. He told me that pigs can suffer from anorexia. Did you know that?

Gillian   I said to Oliver, 'Did Stuart ask after me?'

He looked a bit vague. He was about to reply, then stopped, looked vague again, and said, 'I'm sure he did.'

'And what did you reply?'

'What do you mean?'

'I mean, Oliver, when Stuart asked you about me, you must have answered something. So what did you say?'

'Oh, the usual . . . stuff.'

I waited, which normally works with Oliver. But he just got vague again. Which means either that Stuart never asked after me, or that Oliver can't remember what he said, or that he can but doesn't want to repeat it.

What do you think 'the usual stuff' about me is?

7 : Dinner

Gillian   When I said we fall into bed and don't have sex, you did know it was a joke, didn't you? I should think we have sex about as often as the national average, whatever that is. As often as you do, perhaps. And some of the time it's national average sex. I'm sure you know what I mean. I'm sure you've had it yourself. You may be just about to have it, when you finish this bit.

It goes like this. Not as often as it used to be (and not at all when Oliver was ill). More and more on the same nights every week – Friday, Saturday, Sunday. No, that sounds like boasting. One of the three. Usually Saturday – Friday I'm too tired, Sunday I'm thinking about Monday. So, Saturday. A bit more often in hot weather, a bit more often on holiday. You can't rule out the effect of a sexy film, either, though to tell the truth that seems to work in the opposite way nowadays. When I was younger screen sex used to get my juices flowing. Now I find I sit there thinking, it's not like that – and I don't mean it's not like that for me, I mean it's not like that for anyone else either. So it doesn't work as an aphrodisiac. It still does for Oliver, though, which can cause a problem.

You catch yourself thinking, well, we could always put it off to another time – it's not as if we're going anywhere. That moment of wanting gets more ... fragile, I think. You're watching a TV programme, half-thinking about going to bed, then you change channels, watch some rubbish and within twenty minutes you're both yawning and the moment's gone. Or one of you wants to read and the other one doesn't and he/she lies there in the half-dark waiting for the light to be put out, and then the waiting, the hope, turns to mild resentment, and the moment goes, and that's it. Or, a few days go past – more than usual, anyway – and you find that time works both ways simultaneously. On the one hand you miss sex and on the other you begin to forget about it. When we were kids we used to think that monks and nuns must be secretly randy all the time. Now I think: I bet they don't worry about it at all, most of them, I bet it just goes away.

Don't get me wrong. I like sex; so does Oliver. And I still like sex with Oliver. He knows what I like and what I want. Orgasm is not a problem. We know the best way to get there, for both of us. You could say that was almost part of the problem. If there is one. I mean, we almost always make love in the same way – same amount of time, same length of (horrid word) foreplay, same position, or positions. And we do it like that because that's what works best – that's what experience has told us we like best. So it becomes a tyranny, or obligation, or something. In any case, impossible to get out of. The rule about married sex, if you're interested – and you may not be – is that after a few years you aren't allowed to do anything you haven't done before. Yes, I know, I've read all those articles and advice columns about how to spice up your sex-life, about getting him to buy you special underwear, and sometimes just having a romantic candlelit dinner for two, and setting aside quality time to be together, and I just laugh because life isn't like that. My life, anyway. Quality time? There's always another load of washing.

Our sex-life is . . . friendly. Do you know what I mean? Yes, I can see that you do. Perhaps all too well. We're partners in the act. We enjoy one another's company in the act. We do our best for one another, we look after one another in the act. Our sex-life is . . . friendly. I'm sure there are worse things. Much worse.

Have I put you off? He or she beside you has had their light out for some time now. They're doing that breathing which is meant to sound like sleep but doesn't really. You probably said, 'I'll just finish this bit,' and got a friendly grunt in reply, but then you read on a bit longer than you thought. But it doesn't matter now, does it? Because I've put you off. You don't feel like sex any more. Do you?

Marie   Just Stuart and Pluto the Cat are coming to
dinner.

63

Sophie   Pluto*crat*.

Marie   Pluto the Cat.

Sophie   It's plutocrat. It means having lots of money.

Marie   Just Stuart and Pluto the Cat are coming to dinner.

Stuart   I offered to take them out, but they said there were problems getting a babysitter. I was fairly relieved by the time I got there, because I'd been driving through some pretty unfamiliar pages of the *A–Z*. Where they're living now does not qualify as prime restaurant territory. Nothing but what Oliver in the old days used to call botulism takeaways.

I got lost a few times in the dark and the rain, and started wishing the city had been built on the grid system. Anyway, I finally got to their bit of north-east London. 'Mixed' is one way of describing it. Estate agents might call it 'up-and-coming' and hope not to get sued. Do you still talk about 'gentrification' over here? That used to be the word. But I've been out of the loop for a while. Looking at the street Oliver and Gillian live in, I couldn't make up my mind: were the houses coming up in the world, or the people going down, or the other way around? One house with a burglar alarm, the next boarded up; one with a carriage lamp, the next in multiple occupancy with a landlord who hasn't painted it since the war. There were a couple of skips, but they somehow looked depressing. Is there a word for it when gentrification doesn't work?

They live in the bottom half of a small terrace house: they have the basement and part of the ground floor. The metal handrail wobbled as I went down the steps and there was standing water by the door. 37A was painted on the brickwork in a hand I could tell wasn't Gillian's. Oliver answered the bell, took the bottle from my hand, examined it and said, 'How witty.' Then he started reading out the back label. 'Contains sulfites,' he quoted. 'Tut, tut, Stuart, where are your green credentials?'

Now this is a complex question. I was about to say that while I was theoretically in favour of organic wines, the practicalities were complicated – indeed, I did start saying something along these lines – when Gillian came out of the kitchen. Actually, it's more an alcove or a galley than a kitchen. She was drying her hands on a tea-towel. Oliver immediately started jumping about, doing a fatuous act – 'Gillian, this is Stuart, Stuart, may I present . . .' and so on – but I didn't pay him any attention and I don't think she did either. She looked – she looked like a proper woman, if you know what I mean. I don't mean grown-up – though I do mean that as well – and I don't mean older – though I do mean that as well. No, she looked like a proper woman. I could try and describe her, and what the differences were, but that wouldn't convey things properly because I wasn't

65

standing there making an inventory. I was just sort of taking her in, seeing her again, in a general sort of way, if you know what I mean.

'You've lost weight,' she said, which was nice of her, because most people say, 'You've gone grey,' as a way of breaking the ice.

'You haven't,' I replied, which was pretty feeble, but the only thing I could think of to say at the time.

'Oh yes you have, oh no you haven't, oh yes you have, oh no you haven't,' said Oliver in a pantomime voice.

Gillian had made a delicious vegetarian lasagne. Oliver opened my bottle and pronounced it 'very quaffable', then made approving if patronising comments about the rising quality of New World wines, as if I was a visiting American, or someone he was doing business with. Not that I imagine Oliver does much business.

We caught up on things without getting near any danger areas.

'So how long are you over for?' she asked towards the end of the evening. She wasn't looking at me as she asked.

'Oh, for the duration, I suppose.'

'How long's a duration?' This time there was a smile, but she still didn't look.

'As long as a piece of string,' said Oliver.

'No,' I said, 'you don't understand. You see – I'm back.'

I could tell it came as a surprise to both of them. As I began to explain, the door clicked and a face appeared opposite me. It examined me for a bit and said, 'Where's your cat?'

Gillian   I thought it would be awkward. I thought Stuart would be embarrassed – he used to get embarrassed easily. I thought I might not be able to look him in the face. I knew I had to. I thought: this is a crazy idea, why did Oliver have to ask him round? Why did Oliver have to give me precisely three hours' notice?

It wasn't awkward. The only awkward bit was Oliver flapping about, trying to put us at our ease. Which wasn't at all necessary. Stuart's grown up a lot. He's thinner than he was, and grey hair seems to suit him, but mainly he's just more at ease, more relaxed. Which was surprising under the circumstances. Or perhaps not. After all, he's gone out there, into the world, made his own life, made some money, and here we are, still the same as before except for the children, and being a bit worse off. He could have afforded to be patronising, but he wasn't at all. I got the impression he was slightly impatient with Oliver; no, that's not quite right, it was more as if he was watching Oliver like a cabaret act, waiting for the show to be over before serious business started. I ought to have resented it on Oliver's behalf, but somehow I didn't.

Oliver resented it, though. When I found myself (quite unnecessarily, since it was the first thing I'd said) repeating to Stuart that he'd lost weight, Oliver said, 'Did you know pigs suffer from anorexia?' When I gave him a look, he added, 'Stu told me,' as if that made it any better.

But Stuart just glossed over this, took it as a natural change in the conversation. Apparently it's true that pigs can develop the symptoms of anorexia. Sows in particular. They get hyperactive, they refuse to eat, and they lose weight. What's that about? I asked. Stuart said they didn't really know, but it must be the consequence of intensive breeding. We want our pork lean, but lean pigs are more susceptible to stress. One theory is that stress causes some rare gene to be triggered, which makes the animals behave in the way they do. Isn't that terrible?

'Long pig,' said Oliver, as if this was the story's punchline.

I'd forgotten what a thoughtful person Stuart was. I didn't know what was going to happen with the children, because – well, anyway. I decided on normal bedtimes, so Marie would be asleep – in theory – but Sophie would have half an hour with Stuart if he arrived on time, which of course he did. Sophie's got this rather terrifying knack of asking the wrong question. She's also got this direct manner with people; not at all shy. So after a proper handshake, she looked Stuart full in the face and said, 'We understand you're very rich and you're going to fund some of Daddy's projects.'

As you can imagine, I didn't know where to look – except at Oliver, who was studiously avoiding my eye. I was blushing inwardly, and probably outwardly too, over that 'we' Sophie had used, when Stuart, without missing a beat, and in a perfectly normal tone, said, 'I'm afraid it's more complicated than that. All applications have to go before the board, you see. I'm only one vote among many.'

I was thinking: thanks Stuart, that was kind, thanks for that, when Sophie said, 'You're just fobbing us off.' She had her stern face on.

Stuart laughed. 'No, I'm not fobbing you off. There has

to be a structure, you see. It's all very well being philan-
thropic, but there has to be fairness. And you can't have
fairness unless you have a structure. Can you?'

Sophie looked half-convinced. 'If you say so.'

When she'd gone to bed, I said, 'Thanks.'

'Oh, that. No, I can do corporate-speak. All too well, if
necessary.'

And he left it at that. Just treated Sophie's question like a
child's fantasy, which of course it wasn't.

Later, the door opened a few inches and Marie put her
face through. She said something in a stage whisper. Stuart
was in mid-conversation, and he just paused and gave her a
big wink. It wasn't done for effect, I don't think he could see
that I'd noticed.

He's obviously done well for himself. Not that he talked
about it. Just something about his manner. And he dresses
more smartly. I expect that's his wife's doing. I didn't ask
about her. We kept off that, just as we kept off other danger
areas.

I overcooked the lasagne. I was cross with myself about
that.

Oliver   Another triumph for the Ringmaster. The flick
of my whip persuaded leonine mange and sequinned buttock
to trippety-trip the strobe-lit fantastic. Background music:
Satie's *Parade*. Whose score, as I recall, contains parts for
both a circus whip and a typewriter. Just the symbols that
should be entwined on Oliver's future coat of arms.

Everything went swimmingly. I did not require the

foresight of Nostradamus to guess that Stuart would arrive with a hospitalisable case of lockjaw and the muscular relaxation of an Easter Island statue, but I put him at ease by praising the wine he had so plutocratically furnished for the occasion. Tasmanian pinot noir, would you believe! Gillian was so tense that she cremated the pasta. The kids were great, perfect little ladies both of them. Stuart seemed obsessed by whether or not the neighbourhood was undergoing gentrification, a word he pronounced as if holding it with firetongs. Do you know what that was about? Probably anxiety lest some local Che Guevara liberate the hubcaps from his BMW even as he quaffed and dined.

It's a trifle fuck-striking, the notion of Stuart with a BMW, isn't it? And I was duly fuck-struck as I waved him off on a night as foul as that which saw the return of St Mark's body to Venice. If we believe our Tintoretto. The streetlamps blinked pathetically, while the tarmac gleamed like the rinsed flank of an Ethiope. As he slalomed away in a four-wheel drift, I murmured, 'Auf wiedersehen, O Regenmeister.' The Ringmaster meets the Regenmeister – I wish I'd thought of it earlier.

I have to admit – much as it goes against the grain – that once Stuart got over his initial social trauma, he seemed pretty much at his ease. Rather disgustingly so at times, if you really want to know. Interrupted me on two separate occasions, which would never have happened *dans le bon vieux tems du roy Louys*. What has wrought this genetic modification in my organic chum, do you suppose?

Yes, everything went swimmingly, which is a very

peculiar adverb to apply to a social event, considering how most human beings swim.

Stuart   Oh yes, I asked them how long they'd been vegetarian.

'We're not,' said Gillian. 'Never have been. I mean, we like to eat healthily.' She trailed off, then added, 'We thought you were.'

'Vegetarian? Me?' I shook my head.

'Oliver. You're always getting things wrong.' She didn't say it bitchily, or sarcastically. On the other hand, she didn't say it affectionately either. She said it in a sort of resigned way, as if this was the way matters were, and would be, and it was just up to her to deal with the consequences.

She *has* put on a little weight, hasn't she? But why not? It suits her. I don't like the way they're cutting women's hair very short on the nape nowadays. And I never thought yellow was her colour. Still, none of my business, is it?

Oliver   Stuart did, unwittingly, sing for his supper; that's to say, he throated one pure phrase of Pergolesi in among the Frank Ifield. He was prating on about The Threat to the Universe As We Know It, in other words how biodiversity was going belly up, how modified genes in black turtleneck sweaters would abseil their way into the hitherto protected demesne of Fortress Nature, how the timid songbird would be struck mute and the glossy aubergine lose its sheen, how we would all sprout humps

71

and turn into village grotesques out of Brueghel – not that *that* would be too bad a thing if the alternative were a race of Stuarts – and how genetic modification was a Frankenstein's Monster – at which point I wanted to yodel a note high enough to shatter all the crystalware in the house because the whole *point* of the monster is that he was a real sweetie-pie and no threat to anyone but just unfortunately happened to personify so many of humankind's picayune terrors – but Stuart carried on being boring, boring – as boring as a factory full of power-drills, as some wit put it – about GM – don't you hate acronyms? – and I was about to ask a) what General Motors had to do with the issue, and b) whether the success of Stuart's non-pestiferous greengrocery did not depend precisely upon our fear of the evil gene, and if we took away such fear would the said carrot emporium not go swirling down the U-bend, when he used a phrase that came like the snap of a hypnotist's fingers.

'What did you say?'

Naturally, he told me all the other things he'd said, like a gold-panner crazily displaying his quartz. Finally, his scrabbling fingertips held up the true glister.

'The law of unintended effect.'

He explained that this principle might apply if, for example, the Frankensteined crops turned out to be unpalatable to herbivores, a trait which . . . And so on. But he had lost me, and I was richly lost.

The law of unintended effect. Doesn't that sing out, not like some timid if happily untainted hedgerow warbler, but like a mighty chorus to which humankind, Nature and the Almighty lend their joint voices? (I use the Almighty as a metaphor, you understand. Replace with Thor, Zeus or little Johnny Quark according to taste.) Isn't that just a phrase written in neon? Put it up there alongside 'the word made flesh', *'que sera, sera'*, *'si monumentum requiris, circumspice'*, 'horseman, pass by', 'we have left undone those things which we ought to have done', and 'with trembling hands, he undid her bra'. The law of unintended effect. Does that not explain your life even as it does mine? What metaphysician, what moralist could put it better?

Misunderstand me not. If you are a little less pro-Ollie than you might be – and I suspect you are – you might think my embrace of this refulgent principle exculpatory in some way. As if I'm using it to bleat: not my fault, squire. On the contrary – and leaving present company out of it – I regard it as a true expression of the tragic principle of life. Those old gods are dead, and little Johnny Quark is a grey-suited Stuart of a creation in my book, but The Law of Unintended Effect, now that is grand, that is Greek, that instructs us how mighty is the gap between intention and the deed, between purpose and consequence, how vain our striving proves, how precipitate and Luciferian our fall. We are all, are we not, lost? Those who know it not are the more lost. Those who do know it are found, for they have grasped their full lostness. Thus spaketh Oliver in the Year of Our Quark.

Gillian   Of course, you can have married sex without being married. I suppose that's the worst of both worlds. Sorry, didn't mean to put you off. Perhaps that's what you're just about to have.

8: No Hard Feelings

Stuart   'How did you find my number?' 'Oh, I looked you up in the phone book.' Why do I seem to be having this conversation so often lately? First Oliver, then Ellie. I mean, I know some parts of the UK aren't exactly up to speed, but I was hardly using an advanced system of information retrieval, was I?

Have I been out of the country too long? Possibly. Probably. Like when I went into that antique shop near Ladbroke Grove and said I wanted a small painting but it had to be dirty. The woman gave me an odd look, which was of course quite understandable. No, no, I explained, I want a small painting which *needs cleaning*, at which she gave me an even odder look. Perhaps she thought I thought it'd be cheaper. Anyway, she showed me three or four, and said, 'This one's got a spot of damage as well, I'm afraid.' 'Oh, good,' I replied and settled on that one. She obviously expected me to explain. But that's one of the things I've found as I've got older. You don't have to explain if you don't want to.

It was the same when Ellie came to pick it up. She looked at the apartment, and I didn't explain that. I'd told her my name was Henderson, and I didn't explain that. And I showed her the picture, and didn't explain that. Or rather, I explained that I wasn't going to explain. 'I expect it's rubbish,' I said. 'I don't know about paintings. But I need it cleaned for a particular reason.'

She asked if she could take it out of its frame. It was only then that I started to pay her proper attention. When she arrived, she just looked like one of those million girls in black who seem to have sprung up in England while I was away. Black sweater, black trousers, square-toed wedgy-heeled shoes, little black backpack, hair dyed the sort of black that doesn't exist in nature. Not in England, anyway.

Then she got her toolkit out of her backpack, and though she was doing something quite uncomplicated, something I could have done – cut through the backing strip, ease out some pins, and so on – she did it with such concentration, and such exact use of her fingers. I've always thought that if you want to get to know someone better, you shouldn't take them out for a candlelit dinner, you should watch them at work. When they're full of concentration, only not concentrating on you. Do you know what I mean?

After a bit, I asked her the questions I'd planned. It's obvious she admires Gillian a lot.

75

I found myself thinking, I'm glad your fingernails aren't black too. In fact, they have this thick, shiny, transparent coating. Like the glaze on a painting, I guess.

Oliver   Pub Night again. Reflections upon the metamorphosis of ye tavern. Back before the snows of yesteryear had melted, when the white-ensigned ironclad ploughed the waves, when coinage felt heavy in the palm and royal adultery glamorous, back when Westminster was the sovereign creator of law and the good old English apple contained the good old English worm – back then, a pub was a pub. Behold the sturdy-backed drayman furnishing ale of local fabrication to the mutton-chopped publican, who waters it further before inducing alcoholism in the whey-faced adolescent, the dribbling idiot, the thriftless husband come to piss away the housekeeping, the *mutilé de guerre* with ribboned chest athwart his favourite stool, and the gummy-mouthed senescent clacking away at dominoes in the far corner. The regulars keep their pewter mugs on nails above the bar, a fetid labrador lazes before a spitting fire, and just for a moment – unless the crafty recruiting officer has dropped the King's shilling into your mild and bitter – all is calm and comprehensible in this virile enclave.

Not that I bedizened such places, you understand. The overt frottage of testosterone and the lachrymose sodality of ale – such delighteth not Ollie. But then, at some no doubt identifiable moment, there came the introduction into the public house of the respectable female quaffer – the quaffeuse – the provision of passable food and laughable wine, of pub games, pub comedians, pub strippers, pub sportscreens, of better wine and guidebook food, plus the banishment of piles-inducing oaken furniture – all of which, call it gentrification or genetic modification according to which of Stuart's touchstones you favour, has not displeased Oliver. Snug-bar semioticians may rightly propose the pub as an icon of wider social trends. As the Doge of Westminster recently reminded us, we are all middle-class. Welcome, therefore, O ye tourists, to Bigger Belgium, Greater Holland.

Concentrate, Oliver, concentrate. The pub, if you please. The place, the purpose, the personnel.

Ah, how the voice of conscience resembles, in its cadence and phraseology, the voice of Gillian. Is this what men do? There are many theories as to what it is that men marry – their sexual destiny, their mother, their *doppelgänger*, their wife's money – but how about the notion that what they truly seek is their conscience? God knows, most men aren't able to locate it in the traditional seat, somewhere close to the heart and the spleen, so why not acquire it as an accessory, like a tinted sunroof or metal-spoked steering wheel? Or might it, alternatively, be that this is not what men truly seek but what marriage, of necessity, turns women into? Now that would be rather more banal. Not to mention more tragic.

Concentrate, Oliver. Very well. We were in some luxury tavern – some Beer-Ritz – favoured by Stuart. Fill in the cute and preferably alliterative title of your choice. We were drinking – oh, whatever you would like us to drink. And Stuart – this part I remember well – was being a friend. Or

77

even, Being a Friend. There was, given Stuart, much palaver and rodomontade before he attained his peroration, but his message, as I understood it, had a Yankee simplicity to it: I have succeeded, ergo thou shalt also succeed. How so, O minor Master of the Universe, I ask, my head lolling upon my forepaws like the pub labrador in the old print. I gather he has some business plan or rescue strategy in mind. I subtly imply that I could use a cash injection – I am on the point of comparing myself to a junkie, but draw back, in the presence of one so literal-minded, and suggest instead, more wholesomely, that I need a cash injection as a diabetic needs his insulin. Stuart swore me to campfire secrecy vis-à-vis Gillian; indeed, we might have taken out Swiss Army knives and with nicked thumbs made a pledge of sanguinous fraternity.

'So,' I said, as we settled our flagons back on the quiz-night beer mats, 'No hard feelings? All blood under the bridge?'

'I don't know what you're talking about,' he replied.

So that's all right, then.

Mme Wyatt   Stuart asks me what are soft feelings. I say I do not know what he is talking of. He replies, 'Everyone always says *no hard feelings*, Mme W, so I was just wondering what are soft feelings.' I tell him I have lived here thirty years or more – probably more – but that I certainly do not understand the crazy language. Or the crazy English for that matter.

'Oh, I think you do, Mme W, I think you understand us

78

only too well.' And he gave me a wink. I thought at first it was a nervous tic that had developed, but it clearly was not. This was not the typical behaviour of the Stuart I remember from before.

But then Stuart has changed much. He looks, if it is possible to understand me, like someone who has placed all his troubles behind him in order to embrace with enthusiasm some new ones. He is thinner than he used to be and not so anxious to please. No, that is not quite true. But among men there are different ways of pleasing, at least of trying to please. Some find out what it is that pleases other people and then try to perform it, while others simply do what they propose to do in the expectation and in the confidence that what they have decided to do will in any case please. Stuart has passed from the first type to the second type. For instance, he has conceived of what he calls a Rescue Package for Gillian and Oliver. I do not think that Gillian and Oliver have asked him to rescue them. Is this not the case? So perhaps what he is doing is dangerous. To him, not to them. One is rarely forgiven for being generous.

Stuart does not even appear to be paying attention when I tell him this. He asks me instead, 'Do you know the expression *blood under the bridge?*'

Why am I all of a sudden an expert on the English language? I tell him it sounds like when you punch someone on the nose.

'Hit the nail on the head as usual, Mme W,' he replies.

Ellie   The people you meet in this job – you'd never

79

meet them normally. Like, I'm a 23-year-old picture restorer with just enough money for rent and food, and they're rich enough to have paintings that need restoring. They're quite polite, but they haven't a clue, lots of them. I know far more about pictures than they do, I appreciate them more, but they're the ones that have them.

Take the man whose picture this is. Look, I'll put a better light on it for you. Yes, you said it. Mid-nineteenth-century park railings. He sort of admitted it was rubbish, straight out. If I'd been Gillian I'd probably have said no it isn't just crap it's complete crap, but as I'm not I merely said something about never arguing with a client, and he laughed, but didn't go on to explain. I suppose he could have been left it. By a blind auntie.

The same with how he found me – didn't really explain that. Said he'd looked me up in the book. I pointed out I wasn't in the yellow pages, he said someone had recommended me – who? oh, he couldn't remember – they didn't know the number, blah blah blah. Half the time he was Mr Mystery Man, and half the time he seemed to be really focused.

He lives in this totally bare flat in St John's Wood. You couldn't tell if he'd just moved in or was just about to move out. The lighting was terrible, there were horrible lace curtains, and nothing on the walls – and I mean nothing. Perhaps he'd suddenly noticed and gone out and bought this picture.

On the other hand, he was very interested in the business side of things. Asked me lots of questions about prices, rents, materials, techniques. He somehow knew the right

80

questions to ask. Where our work came from, what we needed in the studio. Said whoever had recommended me had spoken highly of my 'partner'. Boss. So I talked about Gillian a bit.

'I mean, she would probably tell you this isn't worth the canvas it's painted on,' I said at one point.

'Then it's just as well I came to you and not her, isn't it?' He could have been an American who'd lost his accent.

Oliver   The law of unintended effect. You see, when I fell in love with Gillian, I little thought that our *coup de foudre* would exile Stuart to the New Golden Land and translate him into a greengrocer. How little I knew – I didn't even suspect there was a law covering such eventualities. And then – fast-forward a decade – we have the Poussin-esque theme of the Exile's Return. The Friendship Restored. The Happy Trio happy again. The missing jigsaw piece located. I would be pushed to compare Stuart to a Prodigal, but what the fuck, it's somebody's saint's day every day of the year, so here's to St Stuart, raise your goblet and toast this Prodigal Son of ours.

St Stuart. I'm sorry, I gave myself the giggles. Stabat Mater Dolorosa, and crammed into a predella beneath are St Brian, St Wendy and St Stuart.

Gillian   You like Maman, don't you? You probably think she's – what? – a wise old bird, a real character. You probably flirt with her a bit. I wouldn't be surprised. Both

Oliver and Stuart used to, in their different ways. And I bet Maman's been flirting with you, whatever your age or sex. She's like that. She's probably got you round her little finger by now.

It's all right, I'm not jealous. I would have been once. Mothers and daughters – you know the story. And then, mother and daughter without a father – do you know that one too? What the teenage daughter thinks of the mother's . . . suitors, let's call them, what the mother thinks of the daughter's boyfriends. That was a time neither of us likes to look back on. She thought I was too young for sex, and I thought she was too old for it. I went out with some really dirty-looking boys, she went out with pillars of the golf club who wondered if she'd got a few million francs stashed away. She didn't want me pregnant, I didn't want her humiliated. That's what we said, anyway. What we felt was a bit different, less nice.

But that's all over now. We're never going to be like those puke-making mothers and daughters you see in magazines who are always going on about how they're one another's best friend. But I'll tell you what I admire about Maman. She's never felt sorry for herself – or if she has she doesn't admit it. She has her pride. Her life hasn't worked out like she hoped, but she just gets on with things. That doesn't sound much of a lesson, does it? Still, it's what she's taught me. When I was growing up she was always giving me advice and I was never taking it, and the only real lesson I learnt she didn't try to teach.

So I get on with things too. Like when . . . look, I probably shouldn't be telling you this – Oliver would hate it

82

– he'd think it a betrayal – but a year or two back Oliver had his – what? – episode? illness? depression? The words never seemed to cover it at the time and they still don't. Did he tell you anything about it? No, I thought not. Oliver has his pride too. But I remember – vividly – getting home early one day, and he was still lying exactly where I'd left him, on his side, with a pillow over his head so that I could just see his nose and chin protruding, and he could feel my weight as I sat on the bed, but didn't respond. I said – and the words seemed hopeless in my mouth as I uttered them – 'What's the matter, Oliver?'

And he replied, not in one of his jokey voices, but straightforwardly, as if trying very hard to answer my question, 'The inexpressible sadness of things.'

Do you think that's partly it? Inexpressibility, I mean? If depression is the place where words run out, then its inexpressibility must make your plight, your isolation, all the more unbearable. So you bravely say, 'Oh, I'm a bit down', or 'Feeling blue', but the words make it worse, not better. I mean, we've all been there, or nearly there, at some point, haven't we? And Oliver is good with words – as you'll have noticed – so for him of all people to find things inexpressible . . .

Then he added something else, which I remember just as well. He said, 'At least I'm not in the foetal position.' And there wasn't any answer to that either, because it was as if Oliver was saying, 'I know all the clichés as well as you do.' And whatever Oliver is or isn't, he's intelligent, and someone being intelligent about their own depression is unbearable to watch. Because part of you feels their intelligence has helped get them into it but isn't going to be any help getting them out. He wouldn't see any doctors. He calls them the Men Who Guess. Actually, that's what he calls all experts he disagrees with.

And because I'm frightened it might come again, I keep everything organised. I get on with things. I am Little Miss Brisk. Now Mrs Brisk. I think – I hope – that if I keep a structure to our lives, then Oliver can rattle around inside without coming to much harm. I tried to explain this to him once, and he said, 'Oh, you mean like in a padded cell?' Which is why I don't explain things so much any more. I just get on with them.

Oliver   I'm sorry, I had a sudden panic attack. Nothing serious. Just the idea that there really *might have been* a St Stuart. Let's dream his hagiography a while. Goody-goody son of an honest soldier's widow in provincial Asia Minor. While other lads were busy elasticating their prepuces, young Stuartus preferred threading dried beans on a piece of string. Grew up to be a prematurely grey tax-collector in the city of Smyrna, where his pedantic book-keeping uncovered an early Roman scam. The provincial governor's ADC dipping his paw in the grain barrel. The gubernatorial cover-up sadly necessitating the execution of Stuartus of Smyrna on the trumped-up charge of spitting and defecating on idols in the Temple. The local Christian rabble-rousers opportunistically proclaiming him a martyr – whereupon, St Stuart! The law of unintended effect strikes again! Feast Day: April 1st. Patron and protector of the unmodified vegetable.

I hied me to the *Dictionary of Saints*. I was hyperventilating as I flicked the pages. St Simeon the Stylite, St Spiridon, St Stephen (bags of them), St . . . Sturm, St Sulpice, St Susan. Oof! O happy gap. That was a near one.

Call me a name-snob if you will. Call me Oliver. Best mate of Roland. The Battle of Roncesvalles. The seeing-off of the Saracen. A tragic falling out between the chums. Phrase: to give a Roland for an Oliver, *id est*, the exchange of mighty hammer blows in battle. Ah, the age of myth and legend. Charlemagne, knighthood, the high Pyrenean passes, the future of Europe, the future of Christendom itself at stake, the heroic rearguard, the stirring call of the battle horns, the sense of human life, however inconsequential, however much a tiddleywinks counter, being nonetheless flipped into the clash of greater forces. To be a pawn was something indeed when there were knights and bishops and kings on the board, when a pawn might dream of becoming a queen, when there was black versus white, and God above.

You see what we have lost? Nowadays there are only pawns on view, and both sides wear grey. Nowadays Oliver has a chum called Stuart, and that falling-out of theirs does not echo far. 'He gave a Stuart for an Oliver.' Oh dear. Handbags at ten paces.

On the other hand, do you think Hollywood might be ready for *The Song of Roland*? The ultimate buddy movie. Action, scenery, high stakes, and the love of fair women.

Bruce Willis as the grizzled Roland, Mel Gibson as the fabled Oliver.

I'm sorry. I just gave myself the giggles again. Mel Gibson as Oliver. You'll *have* to excuse me.

Gillian   Oliver said, 'Do you think Ellie would suit?'

'Suit what?'

'Stuart, of course.'

'*Stuart?*'

'Why not? He's not that bad-looking.' I just stared at him. 'Thought we could have them both round. Lash out on a saag gosht and a king prawn balti.'

You have to understand that Oliver doesn't really like Indian food.

'Oliver, that's a ridiculous idea.'

'What about combining the two then? Have a saag prawn. Best of both worlds. No? Lamb dansak? Chicken channa? Brinjal bhaji?'

He likes the words rather than the things themselves, you see. I suppose that's a start.

'Aloo gobi? Tarka daal?'

'He's twice her age and married.'

'No he isn't.'

'Ellie's twenty-three—'

'And he's our age.'

'All right, technically—'

'And consider,' said Oliver, 'that with each passing year, he'd become less than twice her age.'

'And he's married.'

'No.'

'You told me—'

'No. Was. Isn't. Free man, not that anyone truly is or can be, as the philosophers have demonstrated with wearisome regularity if different proofs.'

'So he hasn't got an American wife?'

'Not any more. So what do you think?'

'What do I think? Oliver, I think it's just as ...' (nowadays I find myself avoiding words like barmy, potty, mad and the rest) '... as *impractical* as I did before.'

'Well, we've got to find him someone.'

'We do? Why? Did he ask?'

Oliver pouted. 'He'd do stuff for us. We ought to do stuff for him. Be pro-active.'

'Like serve up my assistant?'

'Vegetable samba? Metar paneer?'

Stuart   Blood under the bridge. Like when you punch someone on the nose. Good old Mme W. Or, to be exact about it, like when I head-butted Oliver.

Have you noticed something about Mme W? Her English seems to have got worse. I'm sure I'm not imagining it. She's carried on living here for the last ten years, and instead of her English getting better or staying the same, it's got worse. What do you put that down to? Perhaps as you get older you start losing the things you've learnt as an adult. Perhaps you end up with only what you had as a child. In which case, she'll end up speaking nothing but French.

Gillian   *Impractical* – what a . . . practical word. A
few years ago, I was seriously tempted. I really fancied . . .
this person. I could tell it was mutual. I imagined what I'd
say if he asked me. And I knew I'd say, 'I'm afraid it's
impractical.' And I couldn't bear to hear myself saying it. So
I made sure I never found myself in a place where he'd ask.

Why do you think Stuart didn't tell me he wasn't married
any more? He certainly had the opportunity.

The only reason I can think of is this: he was too
ashamed. Next question: what can there be to be ashamed
of in this day and age, when nobody's judgemental,
whatever sort of failure you make of things? And the only
answer I could think of was this: what if Stuart's second
marriage ended in a way which reminded him of how his
first marriage ended? It's an awful thought, quite awful. I
can't ask him, can I? It's up to him to tell me.

Terri   There are these stone crabs, which I guess you
don't have in your country. What's special about them is
they grow this one big claw, just the one – I mean, the other
stays the normal size. And it's this big claw that's the
delicacy, so the crabbers just tear it off and throw the rest of
the crab back in the water. And you know what the crab
does? It starts growing another big claw all over again. This
is what people tell you, so I suppose it must be true. You'd
think the crabs would just be traumatized, just sink down in
the water and die. Uh-uh. They just keep coming back for
more, as if having their arm ripped off never happened.

As my friend Marcelle says: remind you of something?

9: Curry in a Hurry

Terri   Show the photograph. Get him to show the photograph.

Mme Wyatt   Naturally I am not a *psychologue* or a *psychiatre*. I am just a woman who has examined existence for more years that I hope you will be able to estimate. And one characteristic of the human race which seems to me ineradicable is its capacity to be surprised by unsurprising things. Hitler invades France – surprise! Presidents are assassinated – surprise! Marriages do not last – surprise! The snow falls in winter – surprise!

The opposite would be the surprise. Exactly as it would have been surprising if Oliver had not had some kind of collapse. There is not much solidity to Oliver. He lives on his nerves and frankly is not happy in his skin. Oh, he says he is, of course, he appears pleased with himself, very sufficient, but I have always thought of him as someone who secretly hates himself. Someone who makes a lot of noise because he is terrified of the silence within. My daughter is right when she says that Oliver would be improved by success, but in my opinion that is little probable. His so-called career is a disaster. Well, perhaps not, does not disaster indicate the existence of some initial success, and one cannot accuse Oliver of that. He lives off Gillian, more or less, which is no life for a man. Oh yes, I know the modern theories about how this can be a good idea, the division of work, the flexibility, etcetera etcetera, but the modern theory is only good if the psychology of the person it is applied to is also modern, if you follow.

Is he faithful to Gillian? Don't tell me if you know the answer. I hope he is, of course. But not for why you think – that she is my daughter and infidelity is wrong. No, I think it would be bad for Oliver. There are many husbands – and wives – who are made cheerful by adultery, made better able to bear their lives. Who was it who said that the chains of marriage are so heavy that sometimes it needs three people to carry them? But Oliver is not like that in my opinion. I am not talking of guilt; I am talking of self-hatred, which is quite another matter.

People are surprised that Oliver had a nervous collapse after the death of his father. But he so hated his father, they say. Why did not that death release him from that emotion and make him happy? Well, how many reasons would you prefer? Shall we begin with four of them? One, it is often the case that the death of the second parent revives in the child's mind the death of the first one. Now, Oliver's mother died when he was six, which is a painful experience to endure for a second time, and after such a distance as well. Next, the death of a parent you love is in many ways simpler than the death of a parent you hate or to who you are indifferent. Love, loss, mourning, remembering – we all know the scheme. But what is the scheme when this is not the case, when the parent is not loved? A tranquil forgetting? I think not. Imagine the situation of someone like Oliver, who realises that for all his life as an adult, and for many years before that as well, he has lived without knowing what it is like to love a parent. You will reply that this is not so extraordinary, not so uncommon, and I will reply that this does not make it more easy.

Three, if it is true that Oliver hated his father – I think this is an exaggeration, it was certainly a strong antagonism, but let us call it hate if you will – and if that emotion continued during all his adult life, then perhaps in a sense it had become necessary to him. Perhaps he was sustained by it as certain people are sustained by indignation or sarcasm. So what do you do when it is taken away? Of course you can continue hating the dead person, but part of you will know that this is not reasonable, is even a little bit crazy. And four, there is the question of silence. Your parents are gone, death is coming for you next, you are on your own – even if you have your family, your friends. You are supposed to be adult now, grown up. You are at last free. You are responsible for yourself. You look at that self, you examine it, intimately, finally without the fear of what it is your parents can say or can think. What if you do not like what you see? And now there is a new silence – the silence outside, which is as big as the silence inside. And you – you who are so fragile – you are all that is holding these two great silences apart. You know that when they meet you will cease to exist. Your skin is all that keeps them apart, your thin skin, which has such porosity. Why would you not go a little crazy?

No, it did not surprise me.

Ellie Guess who Gillian and Oliver tried to fix me up with? Or who was at supper, anyway? Mr Mystery Man with no pictures on his wall, aka Mr Henderson. This grey-haired man standing there, then moving towards me a bit quickly and shaking my hand as if we'd never met before. With a look in his eye like, let's keep this a secret. So I went along with it. Which felt more and more weird as I sat there because – guess what? – it turned out he was an old friend of theirs.

So what was the mystery about? If he wanted a picture restorer, why didn't he just ask Gillian?

Still, he was quite interesting. Talked about real things, if you know what I mean. Oliver kept making stupid jokes. So what else is new? I got the feeling there's something about Stuart that really pisses him off. Well, good.

Stuart I read more than I used to. Non-fiction.

History, science, biography. I like to know that what I'm being told is true. From time to time I'll read a novel, if there's one people are going on about. But stories aren't enough like life for me. In stories, someone gets married and that's the ending – well, I can tell you from my own personal experience that this isn't the case. In life, every ending is just the start of another story. Except when you die – that's an ending that's really an ending. I suppose if novels were true to life, they'd all end with all the characters dying; but if they did, we wouldn't want to read them, would we?

What I'm trying to say is this: when I saw – when you and I both saw – Oliver roaring off down that village street in France some ten years ago, you didn't think that was the end of the story? I wouldn't blame you – part of me thought it was too. Maybe I wish it had been. But life never lets you go, does it? You can't put life down the way you can put a book down.

Oliver Stuart, at dinner, was at his most Stuartesque. St Simeon the Stylite would have thrown a wobbly and built his pillar even higher to escape the narcoleptic miasma that encircled the table legs like dry ice. It took me back to the time when – in a vain attempt to get Stu-baby up to speed in matters erotic – I would allow him on double-dates with me. He would sit there with all the animation of a breadstick and mope up a storm when both the signorine chose to be squired home by Yours Truly. I suppose this did furnish the Steatopygous One with some vague social purpose: ease your passage towards troilism by going on a double-date with Stuart! Though there were disadvantages. He used to get all whiney about picking up the bill (*he* should be so lucky), and then you'd have to smoothe his fur and feathers before he pattered off to catch the night bus back to his crepuscular wankpit.

Item: Stuart clearly feels he has upped the *savoir faire* quotient in the last decade. But if on a social occasion you are the only spare male present, it is, is it not, mere good manners to make preliminary enquiries of the only spare female present? As in: 'What do you do for a living?' 'Are you Schedule D or Schedule E?' 'Which tax office do you make your returns to?' But he just stared at Mlle Ellie as if he was having trouble with his contact lenses. After a while I stepped in and provided her brief cv. Which sent him to the opposite extreme, rabbiting on about the global food economy and his mission to vend carrots as authentically gnarled as the Devil's genitalia.

Item: he spent a long time helping Gillian 'clear away'. Rather touching of him to load the dishwasher, but the offstage close-harmony tinkle of forks cascading into their little stacking nooks isn't what I call singing for one's supper.

Item: at one point he came over all rheumy and choleric about the fact that both fiction and non-fiction might hunker down together on the person of sensibility's bookshelf. Furthermore, he railed, why was non-fiction patronisingly defined and named merely in terms of its opposite? Was it not as if fruit were defined as non-vegetables? Or –

just in case we were slow to catch the inference – as if vegetables were defined as non-fruit?

Fiction, I replied, is the Supreme Fiction. Non-fiction is the dross on the fool's gold (whatever that means; but I do like the sound of it). He wasn't following very well. Look, I said, fiction – by which I was naturally referring to art in general – is the norm, the bass line, the golden mean, the meridian, the north pole, the north star, the pole star, the lodestone, the magnetic north, the equator, the *beau idéal*, the summum, the epitome, the ne plus ultra, the shooting star, the Halley's Comet, the Star of the East. It is both Atlantis and Everest. Or, if you wish it more Stuartly, it is the white line down the middle of the road. Everything else is a deviation, a traffic light, a speed camera popping up in your *rétroviseur*.

He thought about this for a while, then chanted, 'You only fit double glazing once, so fit the best – fit Ev-er-est!' Then he grinned at me.

Sometimes my patience is sorely tested. St Oliver, who suffered little bores to come unto him.

Gillian   I couldn't believe it when Oliver told me he'd asked them to supper. Just the two of them, to make it really subtle. I washed my hands of it. Asked what he was going to cook. We had Curry in a Hurry. And, as I said, Oliver doesn't really like Indian food. I can't say I made much of a contribution myself. Stuart did his best. Then he helped me clear up. He stacks dishes with a care that is almost like tenderness. I even noticed him straightening out some of those plastic-covered prongs in the machine, which always end up pointing the wrong way if Oliver goes anywhere near it. At one point he said, not exactly in an undertone, but sort of quietly, yet firmly, 'I think we've got to change this.'

'Stuart,' I said, 'it's a bit old, but it works perfectly well.'

'No, not the dishwasher. The whole thing. You can't go on like this.'

Stuart   My plan is as follows:
  - they all need more space
  - the schools around here aren't up to much
  - Gillian needs a bigger studio
  - Oliver needs to get off his arse
  - so in short they need a decent-sized house in an area where the schools are better
  - funnily enough, I happen to own such a house
  - which is the solution
  - though I can also see it might be a bit of a problem.
I have to persuade Oliver that it's largely for Gill's benefit, and Gill that it's largely for Oliver's. And both that it's better for the kids. Well, that shouldn't be impossible. I softened Oliver up when I last had a drink with him. I think I only wanted to strangle him on two occasions. He got out of control with some silly joke about Beer-Ritz, which he thought was blindingly original. As if there weren't a couple of well-known off-licences in Yorkshire bearing that name already. And then, as we were leaving, he came over all

sentimental as he's inclined to when he's a bit pissed. 'Hey Stuart, me old mucker, no hard feelings, eh? Blood brothers and all that? A Roland for an Oliver, all blood under the bridge, no hard feelings, eh?'

I suspect that Oliver's notion of how I am going to help him contains various elements that are missing from my actual plan.

Ellie   There was a weird moment the other evening. Oliver had been whacking on about art in his usual way, lecturing two of us who actually have degrees or diplomas in the subject, not that he'd notice, and all of a sudden Stuart put on this funny voice and did an ad for double-glazing. From a few years back, by the sound of it. It was surreal. You could see from Oliver's face that he was really pissed off. And if you ask me, Stuart knew exactly what he was doing.

Gillian was a bit frosty with all concerned.

Oliver   Stuart is behaving as if his Famous Plan were designed to pull the tiger economies out of a tailspin. Actually, he's acting more like one of those insufferable Dickensian rescue-package artisans. Usually called Cherry-bum or something equally preposterous.

Mme Wyatt   There is one thing about the return of

97

Stuart which makes me unquiet. Above all, if he becomes involved inside the family again.

You see, Sophie and Marie do not know that their mother was married before.

Absurd, yes? Not of our times, yes?

It was like so. Oliver and Gillian had abandoned their life in England, they had moved to France. Stuart had gone into exile in the United States. The little one – Sophie – was growing up, she was asking all the questions little ones ask. Now my daughter, as you have perhaps observed, is a very direct person. So whatever Sophie asks, she receives the answer. Where babies come from, where the cat goes when he dies, and so on. Well, as it happens, the one question Sophie did not ask because it is not the sort of question that comes into the minds of the little ones, was: just out of interest, Maman, were you ever married to anyone else before you were married to Daddy? So you see, it never arose.

Of course it was more than this. Perhaps it was a way of not thinking about the past. Also, a way of not making life seem too complicated for your child. We all want our children to believe that their point of entry into the world was a strong and a simple matter. Why place difficulties upon the little ones unless they are necessary?

And then it becomes harder to tell what you have not told. And then Marie is born. And you do not expect ever to see Stuart again. But he returns.

Perhaps it does not matter. Perhaps they will laugh together about it one day. Perhaps that is not so likely.

Gillian　　　Look, can we stop this whole business right here?

I said to Oliver, 'Do you realise exactly what Stuart is proposing? He's proposing that we take over the house he and I lived in when we were married to each other.'

Oliver said, 'You mean the house where we fell in love? Entirely appropriate, from my point of view.'

'Why's he still got it after all these years? Don't you think that's peculiar?'

'No, I think it's purely mercantile. He's probably making doubloons out of renting it.'

'So what's going to happen to the tenants? He's just going to throw them out?'

'I think you'll find that if the freeholder wants to repossess with the intention of making the property his principal residence, there's no objection in law.'

'That's not the sort of thing you know.'

'No, it's the sort of thing Stuart knows.'

'Anyway, that's not what's happening. *He's* not going to move in, so he'd be evicting them dishonestly. What would they think?'

'They'd probably think he was being mercantile.'

'Can't you see there's something sick about the idea?'

'Half the house used to be yours. He bought you out. Now you're getting it back.'

'No, I mean sick in that I used to live there with Stuart and now Stuart is proposing that I live there with you.'

'And the children. Anyway, I expect the wallpaper has changed.'

'Is that all you can think about – wallpaper?'

Oliver   Wallpaper, you know, can be so nipple-puck-
eringly poignant. One of my artist-heroes, when in plump
and non-Stuartesque middle-age, found himself visiting the
Mediterranean city where, half a lifetime before, one of his
primal encounters with Venus had taken place. Marseilles,
as memory serves. Erotic nostalgia and wry self-curiosity
sent him questing for that half-forgotten location, but the
quixotries of memory and urban redevelopment betrayed
him. Wearily coming upon a barber's shop, he decided to
abandon his search and have himself shaved instead. Lather
white-bearded his cheeks and the barber was Paganiniing
his strop when, and *tout d'un coup* and *merde alors!*, he
recognised the wallpaper. Faded now, but proof that it had
been here, in this very room, that the tumultuous event had
occurred. Imagine such a moment: the old man's face in the
mirror, the young man's paper on the wall, and in between
the person he then was, assailed by both retrovision and
preview. Must have made the old throat knock against the
razor, eh?

When I told this to Gillian, she asked how my hero could
have been sure it was the same room, as there can't have
been that many different kinds of wallpaper on sale at the
time, and no doubt dozens of houses in the same area must
have had ...

I told her truth sprang directly from poetry.

Stuart   Oliver rang to say that the only stumbling
block for Gillian, as far as he could see, was the wallpaper.
Aren't people odd about where they live?

They'll need another dishwasher. The old one was on its last legs.

Sophie   Daddy says we're moving somewhere nice and bigger. Mummy says we aren't.
I asked if we can afford it, and they pretended not to hear.
So I asked if we could have a cat if we moved somewhere bigger.
They said they'd see about that.

Marie   Pluto the Cat. Pluto the Cat.

Ellie   Oliver rang to tell me that Stuart really liked me but that he was fantastically shy and I might have to make the first move. Oliver spent about twelve minutes wrapping it up. I replied that Stuart seemed a nice enough person, but that middle-aged divorcees weren't exactly my scene. I took about eight seconds to say it and didn't wrap it up.

Stuart   Oliver rang to say that Ellie really liked me but was fantastically shy and I might have to make the first move. I told him that the only 'move' I had in mind was for him and Gillian. He called me various things like a sly dog and said he could tell we really liked one another.
Why does Oliver think I still need his help with the

opposite sex? Not that he was ever much use in the old days. Very occasionally we went on dates together, but he always behaved in such a patronising manner that pretty soon I called it a day. I don't mind being teased, but with Oliver it would degenerate into a sort of drunken aggression. And his idea of helping me was to go on about how much I needed help. Which in the circumstances wasn't helpful.

And I certainly don't need Oliver now. I'm quite capable of noting for myself that Ellie is a young and attractive woman. I also know how to use the telephone.

Another advantage of moving is that they might get a better class of home-delivery curry.

Oliver   Mr Cherrybum sent me a newspaper clipping to the effect that some Government steward might be sent in to 'manage' the local schools, i.e. put down armed rebellion and make drug use optional rather than compulsory. The docent authority hereabouts is apparently on a par with Mr Tim's academy in the matter of product delivery and staff morale.

Look, *I* don't need any convincing. Madame is the decision-maker around here, we all know that. I am a mere Papal State parlaying with Metternich.

Stuart   Oliver told me I had to sort it out with Gillian. That's one from the Department of Unnecessary Advice. We had lunch. The first thing she said, which struck me as typical Gillian, was that she wasn't going to accept charity. I told her I'd been intending to go Dutch anyway.

That's the thing about her: you know where you stand. I realise this might seem an odd thing for *me* to say, given our marriage. But when I look back on it – as I frequently do – I can't see that she actually deceived me. She may have deceived herself, but that's another thing. When I asked her, she told me how things stood. When we broke up, she took the responsibility. When we divided our possessions, she asked for less than she deserved. And I've half a suspicion she wasn't in fact sleeping with Oliver when I thought she was. All in all, you could say she behaved very well. Apart from behaving very badly from my point of view, that is.

So I followed her lead. I said I expected them to pay me a fair rent on the house. Which in turn, I suggested, might concentrate Oliver's mind and persuade him to take what normal people call a proper job. Naturally, as tenants they would in due course acquire the right to buy. Further, I would ensure that the house was in a good state of decoration and repair. This was as near as I got to the vexed question of wallpaper. I mentioned the advantages of better state schools in the neighbourhood. I mentioned that my housewarming present, unless such action was deemed offensive, would be a cat called Pluto. And when I felt, with that instinct you get in negotiation, that one more item, one more offer, would tip the balance, I added – from nowhere, it just came into my head as I spoke – that while I wasn't acquainted with any Hollywood moguls, I might be able to find Oliver a job working for me. As long as that didn't count as charity too. Then I divided the bill fifty-fifty, and the tip the same way too.

She'd come straight from the studio and her shoes had drips of paint on them. They were scarlet, old-fashioned, with a thin strap and a buckle. Tap shoes, character shoes? Something like that. I thought they were rather sweet.

Gillian   Stuart is extraordinarily generous. I mean just that. If he was ordinarily generous, it would be easier to say: no thank you, we'll carry on as we are, we'll look after ourselves, thank you very much. But he doesn't rush in with vague good will, he thinks about what we need, and that's hard to resist. The girls call him Just Stuart, like a sheriff or something. In a funny way it's appropriate: he *is* just.

Oliver says I'm being stubborn and proud, holding out. I don't think it's that. What's at the back of my mind isn't the what but the why. We're all behaving as if Stuart is trying to make amends now that he can afford to. Which isn't the case at all. The opposite is – or ought to be – the case. Oliver doesn't seem to take this in. He somehow assumes that because he, Stuart, has made a success of things, then he, Oliver, ought to benefit. So he thinks I'm being too scrupulous, and I think he's being too complacent. And Stuart's there saying: here's the answer, it's obvious. Is it?

Stuart   The lettings agency thought it might take six months or more to get the tenants out. I explained about moving in myself, but they said proper notice had to be given, and so on. They didn't seem to get my point, so I went round to the house itself. It was a bit strange, going back, but I tried to concentrate on the job in hand. The house is divided into three tenancies. I saw them all separately. I made them an offer. I explained how long it would stay open, and that it was no use to me unless all three tenancies agreed. I was perfectly straightforward about it. Well, I may have invented a pregnant wife returning from the States. Something of the kind.

There's no need to look at me like that. I wasn't throwing orphans out into the snow. I wasn't using a gang of bully-boys. I was just suggesting a deal. It's exactly the same as when you check in for a flight and the plane's overbooked and they offer you a hundred quid if you'll take a later flight. If you're in a hurry and don't care about a hundred quid, you wouldn't give it a thought; if you're a student with lots of time on your hands, it sounds like a nice idea. Money in exchange for inconvenience. You're not obliged to accept, and you don't hold it against the airline.

People understand about deals, they're not shocked by them any more, and they appreciate cash in hand. I told them the law was quite clear about my right to eventual repossession. I agreed it was a nice place: that's why I'd lived there all those years ago and wanted to come back. I emphasised the desirability of a quick solution. I suggested they put their heads together. I had a pretty good idea what would happen. They gave me a No which meant Yes Maybe and which I then converted into Yes Please. I gave them half up front and the other half when they moved out. I asked for a signature. Not for the tax authorities – perish the thought! – just for my own records.

Money for inconvenience. What's wrong with that?

Oliver and Gillian hadn't quite made up their minds, but when I said the house was theirs in thirty days, it did seem to become more of a reality for them. I expected some last, extra condition. There usually is one when people are about to get what they want. It's as if they can't accept the simplicity of the fact, they've got to complicate it, impose their will in some unimportant way. Yes, I'll buy your car but only if you throw in the furry dice dangling from the rear-view mirror.

Gillian said, 'But there's one thing. You aren't allowed to buy us a cat.'

Typical Gillian. Anyone else would ask for more, she asks for less.

'Fine,' I said. And I took the hint. I cancelled the new dishwasher I'd ordered. I decided against having the place redecorated. Just a bit of making good after the tenants left. It wouldn't do Oliver any harm to get down to some DIY.

I also thought, once they're in, I'll leave them to themselves. I've been neglecting my work a bit. Maybe it's time to look for a new pork supplier. I could widen the range of tofu savouries. And what about ostrich? I've always instinctively thought not, but I may be wrong. Perhaps it's time for a customer survey.

Terri   Get him to show the photograph.

10: Condoms

Ellie   Condoms, every time. Every single time until he's had an Aids test and I'm standing at the altar. I only trust what I can see. You would too if you'd known some of the boys I have. And some of the men. Not that men are any more truthful than boys. OK, call them all men for the moment, even the boys, and ask yourself this question: if there was a male pill, one they could take every day, and every time they took it they'd be infertile for a 24-hour period, and if it was them that had to say, 'It's all right, I'm on the pill,' then what percentage of times, when you heard that line, would they be telling the truth? Forty to 45 would be my guess. OK, you're less cynical, you say 60, no you say 80, maybe 90. Maybe even 95. Is that enough? Not for me.

99.99 recurring isn't enough for me. Knowing my luck I'd get the 0.01 that didn't recur.

No. Condoms, every time.

And I don't mean I want to get married. And if I did, it certainly wouldn't be in a church.

Stuart   I don't mind. I mean, there are pros and cons to every method. I don't think it's a big question, unless someone has strong feelings on the matter. As they say, Passion Overcomes All. Or something. It's just a technicality. Really, I don't mind.

Oliver   Argumentation, *per et contra*, by one versed in venery, one slick in the salmon sublety of the heat-seeking spermatozoon, one as familar with man-made barricades as any Communard.

1) The French letter, English overcoat, or (as our Slavic cousins so depressingly put it) the galosh. Indeed, something of the rubber overshoe does hang about this device. Call me an aesthete if you dare, but consider the ramifications – semiotically, psychologically – of the man who puts a teat on the end of his todger. And while its presence may furnish comfort and resolve to those of a hair-trigger disposition, the aftermath has always struck me as adorned with *tristesse*. That first moment of withdrawal, the fingers nervously locating the thickened quoit, and then the long lubricated pull. Why am I always reminded of those prisoner-of-war films when the escape tunnel has collapsed

and the smothering RAF officer has to be hauled out by his heels? And then, to be presented with the dangling evidence of one's deed, as an infant is proudly shown its potty. A lightning strike of cosmic melancholy is appropriate at that moment, surely?

2) The diaphragm, cap or (that extinct flightless South American bird) the pessary. Waiting out the inamorata's visit to the bathroom – always a detumescing blip on the graph of action. The longbow is drawn and taut, the archer straining at his aim, when Henry V – or, more likely, Bardolph – orders him to return the arrow to the quiver *pro tem*. Ah well, time to hum a little gamelan music to oneself *en attendant*. Then there is the question as to whether lingual delight is enhanced or not by the flavour of lubricating gel. For a rare and happy few, perhaps it is.

3) The pill. Ah, flesh on flesh, the careless rapture, the shame-free Adam-and-Eveing of it all. As the motorist's life was transformed by the self-starter, so was the sensualist's by the pill. After that, everything else felt like hand-cranking.

4) What is called the female condom. No personal knowledge or experience here, but is it not, must it not, be like fucking a groundsheet? Perhaps useful for those fetishised by early scouting experiences.

5) Vasectomy. It's the -ectomy that puts me off.

6) Non-penetrative sex. Waiter, I'll have the three-course dinner, please. An amuse-gueule, a palate-cleansing sorbet, and a decaf espresso.

7) Semi-penetrative sex, time-delay systems, karezza, withdrawal, mutual masturbation, sleeping naked with a

sharpened sword between you, Scotch love (as the French wittily denote dry-humping), twin beds, chastity belts, celibacy, the Gandhi option . . . all that impedes the true meeting of true bodies: forget it. For-fucking-get it.

Gillian   It's always a compromise, isn't it? I mean, unless you're doing your best to get pregnant. The pill made me feel bloated. The coil made me bleed more than usual, and I never quite trusted it since the day a friend's Copper 7 came out with the placenta of her first child. So it's the old choice between condom and diaphragm. Oliver hates condoms. Actually, it's more that he isn't all that good at using them (which is why he hates them). And there's something a bit passion-killing about Oliver cursing and struggling from the other side of the bed – almost as if it was *my* fault – and on more than one occasion flinging the thing across the room in a pet. For a time we solved this by me putting them on him. He liked being mothered in this way. But that was around the time he got depressed, and he sometimes – well, quite often, actually – used to lose his erection in the middle of things. Which used to make *me* anxious as well, in case, you know, it fell off inside me.

So that leaves the diaphragm. Which isn't perfect. But at least I'm in control. Which is what I want. And, I think, what Oliver wants.

Oliver   Meant to say. When we lived in France.

Buying condoms. You ask for *préservatifs*. Monsieur Druggist, it's the jam-making season again. A sachet of preservatives if you please. Odd that a Catholic country should make them sound like life-savers, when in fact they are the opposite. 'Packet of sperm-assassins, please': that's what you'd expect, wouldn't you? What are they meant to preserve? The health of the mother, the boiler pressure of the father?

Terri   I guess it was a year or so into our marriage. Before we saw the therapist, anyway. I date it to the time Stuart started getting in shape. The step machine in the apartment, trips to the gym, Sunday-morning jogging. Stuart taking his pulse while the sweat broke out on his forehead. It was kind of cute in a way. It was a health thing. I suppose that's obvious. What I mean is, I thought at the time it was only a health thing.

He didn't like me being on the pill full time. We had a few jokes about genetic modification and preferring organic produce, and so forth. He suggested the morning-after pill. Lower hormone dosage into the body, no interference with sex-life: made sense. I'd been using it a couple of months when one Sunday morning I can't find my pills. I'm not the tidiest person in the world, but there's always a few things a woman knows where she keeps and one is control of her own fertility. Stuart is pretty calm about it, and I'm getting a little crazy and end up calling drugstores to see who's open and driving halfway across town. Actually, Stuart's driving, and I'm going Faster, faster, and he says, It doesn't work like that, but I don't think either of us knows. I'm worried that when the car hits a bump it will, like, help things on their way.

A few days later, I find my pills, underneath some Kleenex. How did they get there? Brain damage, I think. A couple of months go by, another Sunday morning, again I can't find my pills, and like the last occasion, I realise it's really high-risk time. Stuart's up already, on his step machine, and I just rush at him and go, 'Did you hide my fucking pills, Stuart?', and he's Mr Calm, Mr Sensible, and swears he hasn't and just carries on stepping up and stepping down, and then he reaches for his pulse and I just lose it. I push him off the machine and go downstairs in my robe and bare feet and get in the car and head across town to the drugstore. The same clerk serves me, and he gives me an eyebrow, like, Lady, get your *life* together. So I do and I go back on the pill. The before pill, the always pill.

Mme Wyatt   *Quelle insolence!*

11 : Not a Bowerbird

Stuart   Gillian told me, in strictest confidence, that Oliver had a bit of a mini-breakdown after his father died. I said, 'But he hated his father. He was always going on about him.' Gillian said, 'I know.'

I thought about this for a long time. Mme Wyatt gave me a complicated explanation in several parts. I gave her a much simpler one: Oliver is a liar. Always has been. So maybe he didn't really hate his father, just pretended to in order to get sympathy. Maybe he really loved him, so when he died Oliver felt not just grief but guilt at having slagged him off all those years, and the guilt provoked the breakdown. How about that?

What did Gillian say, when I went to dinner with them? 'Oliver, you're always getting things wrong.' That's from someone who knows him inside out. He thinks the truth is bourgeois. He thinks lying's romantic. Time to grow up, Oliver.

Terri   He still hasn't shown the photograph, has he? Do you think a subpoena will work?

Stuart   And while we're clearing things up: Terri. I was married to Terri for five years. We got on. It just didn't pan out. I didn't treat her badly or anything. I wasn't unfaithful. Nor was she, I hasten to add. She had a slight problem with . . . the previous incumbent, but that was all. We got on. It just didn't pan out.

Terri   You see, basically what I was up against with Stuart was all that fucking reasonableness. He comes on like this nice, normal guy. And that's not wrong, so far as it goes. He's straight with you, he's honest – up to the point where he can't see when he's being dishonest. So what else is new? I don't know how far he's a typical Brit, so I don't want to put down, like, the whole nation. But he's about the most secretive guy I've ever met, emotionally, I mean. You ask Stuart to talk about his needs and he looks at you as if you're some kind of New Age kook. You ask him to define his expectations of a relationship and his face is like you've said something obscene.

Look. The evidence. The photograph. I need some

money. Stuart tells me to take a fifty from his wallet, a photo falls out, I look at it, I say, 'Stuart, who's this?' He goes, 'Oh, that's Gillian.' The first wife. Yeah, sure, why shouldn't he, and all that. In the wallet, two, three years into our marriage, well, why not? I've never seen her picture before, but, hey, why should I have?

'Stuart, is there anything you'd like to tell me about this?' I ask.

'No,' he says.

'Sure?' I say.

'No,' he says. 'I mean, that's Gillian.' He takes the photo and puts it back in his wallet.

I book the marriage therapist, naturally.

We last about eighteen minutes. I explain that basically my problem with Stuart is getting him to talk about our problems. Stuart says, 'That's because we don't have any problems.' I say, 'You see the problem?'

We chase that around the block for a while. Then I say, 'Show the photograph.'

Stuart says, 'I haven't got it.'

I say, 'But you've carried it around with you every day for the whole of our marriage.' I'm guessing, but he doesn't deny it.

'Well, I haven't got it today.'

I turn to the therapist, who is a) a woman, and b) the least flakey person in the world, and therefore c) chosen to help Stuart take the lid off himself a little, and I say to her, 'My husband carries around with him in his wallet a photo of his first wife. It's in color, and it's a little out of focus, and it's been taken from above, from an angle, I guess, with a long

115

sort of lens, and it shows his wife, his ex-wife, looking terrified, with blood on her face, as if she's been beaten up, and she's holding a baby, and to be honest when I saw it I thought she was a refugee from a war zone or something, but it's just his ex-wife looking like she's screaming, with blood on her face, that's all. And he carries it around with him. Every day of our marriage.'

There was a long pause. Finally Dr Harries, who has been strictly neutral, strictly non-judgemental for like sixteen minutes, says, 'Stuart, would you care to speak to that?'

And Stuart says, in his most tight-assed way, 'No, I wouldn't care to.' And he gets up and leaves.

'What do you make of that?' I ask.

The therapist explains it's a rule of the practice that both partners have to be present before she will make any comments or suggestions. All I'm asking for is an opinion, a simple fucking opinion, but I don't even get that.

So I leave, and I'm not at all surprised that Stuart is waiting in the car for me and he drives me home while we talk about the restaurant. As if he hadn't taken offense – which in a way he hadn't, I suppose. He just wanted out of there.

I give it one more try, later that day. I say, 'Stuart, did you do that to her?'

And he says, 'No.'

I believe him. I mean, it's important to say that. I absolutely believe him. I just don't know him. Who's in there? He'd be a great guy to love if you didn't need to ask yourself that question.

Oliver   Do you remember Mrs Dyer? My concierge and Cerbera at number 55 when I roosted across the road from the newly nuptualised Hugheses (how I hated that plural). There was a diseased monkey-puzzle tree in the front garden, and a gate that winced and ailed. I offered to mend it, but she claimed that there was nothing wrong with it. Unlike *moi*. I was bruised and she tended me. The pages of her own life were by now well foxed; her head sat on her spine like a drooped sunflower upon its stalk; her white hair was reverting to biscuit. I would gaze tenderly upon her incipent tonsure, a breathing hole in a pie-crust.

A sudden fear: might she be dead, replaced by some confident young couple who have rehued her ochre door, hung cheery Roman blinds in her windows and levelled the tree to make off-road parking for the family space-wagon? Oh, please be there for me still, Mrs Dyer. The deaths of those we have known but passingly strike a different note, the celeste rather than the mighty tubular bell, yet they are a surer mark of time's relentless betrayal. The deaths of those close to us may well be the 'life events' beloved of The Men Who Guess; but the deaths of those who enter but fleetingly the orchestral score of our lives make us whiff the marsh gas of mortality.

I hope to God that Mrs Dyer is still alive. May her monkey-puzzle flourish like the green bay, and may that sunflower head lift heliotropically when Oliver stirs her intermittent doorbell.

Gillian   'I wonder who lived here before,' said Sophie.

'Different people,' was all I could think of as a reply.

'I wonder where they've gone,' she added. It wasn't a question, any more than her first remark had been, but I felt defensive. I also felt, suddenly, Stuart should be here; he'd know the answer to that, after all the whole thing was his idea. He got us into this.

No, we got us into this.

No, I got us into this.

One of the ways I deal with it is to go out into the street and look up and down. You know the kind of street this is: a hundred or so houses, fifty on either side, in terraces of twenty-five at a time, all part of a late-Victorian development, all indistinguishable. Tall, thin terrace houses of that yellow-grey London stock brick. Semi-basement, three storeys, with an extra room on each half-landing. Tiny front garden, thirty-foot back garden. What I tell myself is, this is just one of a hundred identical houses in the street, one of a thousand in the neighbourhood, one of a hundred thousand or more across London. So what does the number on the door matter? The bathroom and kitchen are different now, the decoration's changed, I'm not going to have my studio on the top floor as I did before, but on the middle so it won't feel the same, and if there's anything that reminds me of ten years ago I'll get out the paintbrush. The girls help make the house feel new. And a cat would be a good idea, I think. Anything that's new would be a good idea.

If you want to say I'm evading things, perhaps I am. But at least I know what I'm doing. Anyway, that's how you live after a while, isn't it, how everyone lives? Evade a few things, ignore a few things, keep away from certain subjects.

That's normal, that's grown-up, that's the only way to live if you're busy, if you've a job, if you've children. If you're young, or you haven't got a job, or you're rich, if you've got either time or money or both, then you can afford to – what's that word? – confront everything, examine every aspect of your relationships, question exactly why you're doing exactly what. But most people just get on with things. I don't ask Oliver about his projects and I don't ask him about his moods. In return, he doesn't ask me if I'm feeling hemmed in or frustrated or exhausted or whatever. Well, perhaps he doesn't ask because it doesn't cross his mind.

Outside the back door there's a newish bit of red-brick patio, which wasn't there before, the old grass, which is neutral enough, and a pretty unco-ordinated mixture of plants and shrubs. Yesterday I went out and cut down the only two shrubs I remembered from ten years ago. I recognised them because I'd planted them myself: a buddleia, in the hope of attracting butterflies, and a *Cistus ladanifer*, another act of optimism. I cut them down to the ground and then I dug up the roots. I made a bonfire and burnt them. Oliver was out with the girls and when he returned he saw what I'd done but didn't comment.

That's what I mean, you see.

Stuart seems to be just letting us get on with it. He sent us a leg of pork as a house-warming present.

Ellie   The new studio's much better. More room, more light. There would have been even more light if we'd been on the floor above. Also, less noise from the rest of the house. But I suppose that's why they wanted their bedroom on the top floor. Anyway, it's none of my business.

I've just finished Stuart's picture. It didn't improve with cleaning, that's for sure. Having it here became a bit embarrassing. I'd find myself working on it when she wasn't around. Once she gave it a glance, as if to say, 'Cheaper to put it on the fire.' I made a sort of noise agreeing and put my head down. 'It belongs to Mr Henderson,' I said to myself, in case I had to say it to her.

I rang Stuart on his mobile, as he'd asked me to. He said bring it round and we'll have a drink. Not exactly an invitation, not exactly an order, just a sort of statement. I told him what the bill would be.

'You'd prefer cash,' he said, again in the same way. I wasn't being pushed, but I wasn't being asked either. I didn't exactly take offence, I just felt he was in the adult world and I wasn't. The way he was behaving must seem perfectly normal to him and lots of other people, but not to me. I suppose you get used to it, you call it the way of the world or something. Only, I'm not sure I want to get used to it. Ever.

Stuart   Pigs are highly intelligent animals. If you submit them to stress, by overcrowding for instance, then they tend to mutilate one another. It's the same with chickens – not that chickens are particularly bright. But pigs get stressed and attack one another. They chew one another's tails off. And you know what the industrial farmer's response to this is? He docks the pigs' tails so they won't have anything to chew, and sometimes their ears as well. He also clips their teeth and puts rings in their noses.

Now, none of this is exactly going to reduce a pig's stress, is it? Nor is being pumped full of hormones and antibiotics and zinc and copper, and not being allowed to wander about a field or sleep on straw. Things like that. And apart from anything else, stress affects the relaxation of the muscles, which in turn affects the taste of the meat. So does the pig's diet, of course. People in my business agree that pork is the meat that's lost the most flavour as a result of factory-farming methods. And because it doesn't taste of anything, consumers have to be charged less for it, and that drives down the production margins, and so on. Getting the consumer to pay more for decent pork is a bit of a crusade with me, if you must know.

The other thing it makes me think – well, the whole organic argument makes me think – is, what about us? Isn't it exactly the same with us? How many people live in London? Eight million? More? With animals, at least the experts have worked out how much space each of them needs, if they're not to get stressed. They haven't even started to do this for people – or if they have, we don't take any notice. We just live on top of one another, higgledy-piggledy – is that where the phrase comes from? – and bite off one another's tails. We can't imagine things being different. And given our stress levels and what most of us eat, I bet we taste horrible.

Look, this isn't a comparison. It's not one of Oliver's

comparisons, at any rate. It's just a logical progression of thought. It makes sense, doesn't it? Organic human beings – what a difference that would make.

Gillian   I'm looking down from the bathroom window into the garden. It's a beautiful morning, just a touch of autumn in the air and the light. There's a sparkle of dew on a spider's web across the corner of the window. The children are in the garden, playing. It's one of those mornings when even an array of London back gardens, half of them untended, separated by low yellow-grey walls, a few blighted trees here and there, a few plastic climbing frames here and there – when even an ordinary view like that can seem pretty. I look back to the girls and they're running in a circle, half-chasing one another, just having fun. They're running round a pile of ash.

I think: three days ago I cut down two shrubs – shrubs I liked, which I'd planted myself – because of what happened in this house ten years ago. I took it out on the shrubs. I hacked them down, grubbed them up and set fire to them. At the time, it seemed an entirely sensible, practical, logical, reasonable, necessary thing to do. Now, as I watch my daughters dance around what's left of a couple of plants I decided to punish, it strikes me as almost the behaviour of a mad person. Doctor, I left my first husband for my second husband, so ten years later I incinerated a buddleia and a cistus. Can you give me anything for this sort of behaviour?

I know I'm completely sane myself. I'm just saying, some

small, neutral action – some action that doesn't harm anyone and never will – can seem quite sane one day and quite mad the next.

Marie's just tripped and fallen into the ash pile, and since Oliver isn't here I'll have to go down and clean her up. At least all of *that* is sane.

Oliver My first neighbourly duty – no, more an attempted appeasement of existential panic – was a call at number 55. The windows still suffered painfully from glaucoma, and the monkey-puzzle middle-fingered its bottle-brushes at me from the front garden. The door was still the same shade of *caca de dauphin*. No pigment modification – might she yet live? The pad of my forefinger, cruising on muscle memory, found just the right nor'-nor'-easterly angle from which to press the bell. Was ever pause so pregnant? Was ever pregnancy so hysterical? But then I heard the slippered slide of ancient feet.

As with the revisited domiciles of childhood, so Mrs Dyer was even smaller than I had remembered. All that emerged into the sunlight was a downturned crown and a contorted extremity which looked as if it had received a visit from the footbinder. To facilitate our reacquaintance, I fell to my knees as once I had when offering her my hand in marriage. Even so, my head felt high enough to nestle in her shoulder. I revealed my identity, whose specificity alas appeared to evade her. Eyes as milky as the windows surveyed me. I talked of incidents she might recall, laid out my carvery table of jokes in the hope of attracting the inquisitive prod of her fork. But none seemed to her taste. In point of truth, she responded as if I were barking mad. Well, at least she was alive, after a fashion. I rose from my knees like a *cavaliere-servente* and bade her farewell.

'Eleven twenty-five,' she said.

I looked at my watch. She was several hours out, unfortunately. But then, I reflected, perhaps this is the nature of time: the less there is of it left, the less you care about its calibration. I was just deciding not to tell her the news that the sun was nearly over the yardarm when she repeated, 'Eleven twenty-five. That's what you owe me for the gas.'

Then she withdrew her swaddled foot and slammed the door.

Mme Wyatt   Stuart tells me that he is happy to be returned in England.

Stuart tells me that the friendship is restored.

Stuart tells me that Sophie and Marie are charming children and he almost feels like a godfather to them.

Stuart tells me he will try to get Oliver an employment in his business.

Stuart tells me that he is only anxious about Gillian, who seems to him to be under stress.

I do not believe all of this, of course.

But it does not matter so much what I believe. What matters is how much of it Stuart himself believes.

Stuart   And I was also thinking this. Do you know what I mean by ADI and MRL? No? Well, you ought to. ADI is acceptable daily intake. MRL is maximum residue limit. MRL is about the amount of pesticide allowed by law in food when it leaves the farm gate. ADI is about how much pesticide we can absorb into our bodies without it doing us any harm. They're both expressed in mg/kg, that's to say, milligrams per kilogram. In ADI the kilogram obviously refers to our body weight.

This is what I was thinking. When people live together, some of them produce the equivalent of pesticides which are harmful to others. For instance, horrible prejudices which just seep into those around them and poison and pollute them. So I sometimes look at people, at couples, at families, in terms of pesticide level. What's the MRL of him over there, I ask myself, that fellow who's always sneering and full of nasty opinions? Or, if you lived with her for any length of time, what would be your ADI? And what about your kids? Because when it comes to absorbing poisons kids are more susceptible and vulnerable than adults.

I think I've got just the job for Oliver.

Sophie   Yesterday I found Mum in that room at the back of the house, the one above the bathroom, that we don't know what we're going to use for yet. She was just standing there, miles away. She didn't even notice me. It was a bit creepy because she usually notices everything. But she's been a bit odd ever since we moved in.

'What are you doing, Mum?' I asked. Sometimes I call her Maman, and sometimes I call her Mum.

She was a million miles away. Then she started looking round and eventually she said, 'I was wondering what colour to paint it.'

I hope she isn't getting Down in the Dumps, like Dad did.

Ellie   I took back the picture. His flat looked exactly the same, except for about twenty shirts in dry-cleaning bags on a table in the sitting-room. It all looks so temporary. Except if it *was* temporary, it would look more permanent, if you know what I mean. If he was some businessman working in London for a few months, he'd be in one of those flats you see advertised in the free magazines that come through the door. Three-piece suites, standard lamps, swagged curtains hooked back with belts, inoffensive prints on the wall. He saw me looking.

'Don't have time, really,' he said. 'Or maybe it's I've got the time but I don't have the taste.' He thought about it some more. 'No, I don't think it's that either. It's more that I don't have the taste just for myself. It seems rather pointless. If it's just for me, then I don't want it enough to get interested. I want someone else to want it. I think that's it.'

He could have made all this sound pathetic, but he didn't. It was more like he was trying to get to the bottom of it. 'What about you?'

I told him how I went about decorating my bedsit, where I got the stuff. When I said 'charity shop', he looked as if I said I got things off a skip.

'I can't imagine going to that trouble,' he said. 'Do you think it's a sex difference?' No, I don't, actually. 'Do you think it's genetic?'

We'd both seen this wildlife programme on the telly, a few days before, about bowerbirds. Did you watch it? They live in the jungle somewhere, south-east Asia, I think, and the males spend vast amounts of time and energy creating display areas to attract females. They arrange all these flower blossoms and small nuts and pebbles and things in huge piles and swathes. It looks like some naïve artist's been at work. I mean, they're not nests or homes or anything, they're just displays to attract the female of the species. It was all very beautiful, and at the same time I found it a bit scary, the amount of obsessive activity and artistic purpose that basically went into getting a shag.

I didn't say that last bit, but when we'd finished talking about the programme we both found ourselves looking round his flat and laughing. Then he got up and sort of rearranged his shirts on the table, standing some of them up and colour-co-ordinating them, like it was a display. It was quite funny.

'You wouldn't have time for a quick drink? There's a pub on the corner.'

This time he asked it normally, not like on the phone, so I said yes.

Stuart   Why do we like people? This one rather than that one, I mean.

As I think I said before, when I was growing up, I used to

like people because they liked me. That's to say, I would like them enormously if they were merely polite and decent to me. Lack of self-confidence. That's often why people get married the first time, if you ask me. They can't get over the fact that someone seems to like them, no questions asked. There was a bit of that in my case with Gill, I can see that now. It's not enough of a basis for things, is it?

Then there's another way of getting to like people. You see it in those classic serials on telly. For instance, a man and a woman meet and she doesn't particularly rate him, but over a period of time he performs various actions which make her realise that he's a really decent fellow after all, and then she does like him. You know, Lieutenant Chadwick rescues Major Thingummy from a gambling debt or some potentially ruinous position or some social or financial embarrassment, whereupon the Major's sister Miss Thingummy, who Lieutenant Chadwick has admired without getting anywhere with ever since being posted to the region, suddenly recognises his virtues and *likes* him.

I wonder if things ever happened this way, or if it's just a fantasy on the writer's part. Don't you think it's the other way round? In my experience, for what it's worth, you don't meet someone, then be given a certain amount of evidence about them, and on the basis of that decide that you like them. It's the opposite: you like someone and then go looking for evidence to support that feeling.

Ellie's nice, isn't she? You like her, don't you? Do you have enough evidence? I like her. Perhaps I'll ask her out properly. Do you think that would be a good idea?

Would you be jealous?

Oliver   Mr Cherrybum maintains that everyone – from hoi polloi to high pontiff – needs a Business Plan. He even had the *culot* and the *cojones* to ask what mine was. I pleaded flagrant ignorance. The music-drama of till and vault may vitalise Stuart's soul, but not mine.

'All right, Oliver,' he said, setting his elbows firmly on the quasi-marble pub table-top. He temporarily eschewed his beaker of King & Barnes Wheat Mash (you see, I can have an eye for quotidian detail if I wish) and looked at me, I was going to say man to man, but – forgive the chortle – I don't think either of us qualifies. And I don't think I want to, given the grim viva voce involved, the medical inspection and the assault course, the perils of bonding. I can hear the campfire bonhomie, feel the flick of a wet towel. No, I wish to be excused. Here's a note from my mum. She never wanted me to grow up to be a man.

'Let's start at the beginning,' he said. 'Who do you think you are?'

My friend does exhume the sempiternal philosophical posers, doesn't he? Nevertheless, the question deserved answer. '*Un être sans raisonnable raison d'être*,' I replied. Ah, that old poet's wisdom. Mr C looked puzzled. 'A being with no reasonable reason for being.'

'That's as it may be,' said Stuart. 'We none of us know why we have come to this great vale of tears. But it's no excuse for not getting on with the job, is it?'

I explained that this was precisely the reason for not getting on with the job, the irrefutable justification for accidie, excess of black bile, Melancholicke Disease, call it what you will. Some of us arrive in the vale of tears and feel disinherited by Fate; others – I leave you to guess – immediately get out their daypack, fill their waterbottle, check their supply of Kendal mint cake, and stride off up the first footpath they see, ignorant of where it leads, yet convinced that they are somehow 'getting on with the job', and confident that a pair of waterproof trousers will be protection enough against earthquake, forest fire and carnivorous raptor.

'You have to have a goal, you see.'

'Ah.'

'Something to aim at.'

'Ah.'

'So what do you think it might be, in your case?'

I sighed. How to translate the inchoate stirrings of the artistic temperament into a Business Plan? I gazed into Stubaby's Wheat Mash as if into a crystal ball. Very well then. 'Nobel Prize,' I offered.

'I'd say you've still got a very long way to go.'

There are times, wouldn't you agree, when Stuart really hits the nail on the head? That bruised and blackened left thumb is evidence of his more habitual aim, but once in a while, Stuart, once in a while . . .

Stuart   Every so often I start making a list. *Liar, parasite, wife-stealer*, it usually begins. *Pretentious berk* is normally the next item. Then I stop myself. I mustn't let Oliver provoke me, least of all when he doesn't know he's doing it. There are feelings which don't have any point to them, which don't have anywhere to go. And because they don't have anywhere to go, they can get out of hand.

We had a very sensible discussion, interspersed as it was by bouts of facetiousness from Oliver. I managed to ignore them because what I'm doing is for those two girls. And for Gill. So it doesn't really matter what Oliver thinks or says. As long as he does what's best for them.

Oliver is to be my Transport Co-ordinator. Starting on Monday. It's a new position I've created specially for him. He might have to put some of his other ambitions temporarily on hold, but I think having a proper job will help him grow up. And that, in turn, might help those other ambitions of his.

Oliver   Long ago, in the kingdom of dreams, when the world was young and we were young with it, when passions were high and the heart pumped blood as if there were no tomorrow, when Stuart and Oliver felt momentarily like Roland and Oliver, so that half a London postal district resounded to the thud of knobkerrie on breastplate, the said hero, yclept Oliver, confided the following Thought for the Day to . . . well, to *you*, if truth be served. And truth must be served, even if on my menu it requires wholegrain mustard, some pungent garnishings and a few fantastical side dishes to make it palatable. At the time, I confessed to you that my proposed resolution to the then *imbroglio* went as follows:

Stuart has to step down. Oliver has to step up. Nobody

must get hurt. Gillian and Oliver must live happily ever after. Stuart must be their best friend. That's what has to happen. How high do you rate my chances? As high as an elephant's eye?

I could see from your expression at the time – sceptical to the point of faroucheness – that you judged this the landscape of invention, as verisimilitudinous as operetta. Yet was I not as far-seeing as St Simeon the Stylite atop his pillar at Telanissus? Hath not it come to pass just as I spake, O ye of little faith?

It was said of the ascetic and eremitic Simeon that 'despairing of escaping the world horizontally, he tried to escape it vertically'. The pillar on which he dwelt was at first no higher than a bird table, but over the years he built it ever more heavenwards, until this upwardly mobile home was sixty feet tall, equipped with both platform and balustrade. Now, the seeming paradox of his life was that the further he distanced himself from *terra firma*, the greater his wisdom grew, so that petitioners for counsel and solace arrived in ever greater numbers. A pretty parable of sagacity and its attainment, *n'est-ce pas*? Only by distancing yourself from the world do you see it clearly. The ivory tower has been much maligned, no doubt because of its luxury cladding. You leave the world in order to understand the world. You escape into knowledge.

Au fond, this is why I have for decades been a resilient opponent of what those of a parental or admonitory nature have termed a regular job. And now – Lordy, Lordy – St Simeon the Van Driver.

I told Stuart I wanted to be paid in cash. He was obviously impressed that I had the makings of a Man with a Plan. He smiled and extended his paw. He might have said, 'Put it there, pal.' He might have winked in a horribly complicit manner. At any rate, he made me feel like a freemason. Or, more exactly, like a person trying to pass himself off as a freemason.

12: Wanting

Stuart   You don't get things by not asking for them.
You don't get things by not wanting them, either.

That's another difference. When I was younger, I got
what I was given. That's what life seemed to be about. And
in the back of my mind I assumed that there was some
system of justice up there. But there isn't. Or if there is, it's
not for the likes of me. Or you, probably. If we only get
what we are given, then we don't get much, do we?

And it's all about wanting, isn't it? When I was younger
there were lots of things I pretended to want, or assumed I
wanted, simply because other people did. I'm not claiming
to be older and wiser – well, only a bit – but nowadays I
know what I want and I don't waste time on what I don't
want.

And if you're on your own, you don't have to worry about someone else wanting something. Because that takes up a lot of time too.

Ellie   Stuart is not a bowerbird. Sorry, it just makes me laugh when I say it.

I said to him, 'Where are you going to hang it?'

He said, 'Hang what?'

'The picture?'

'What picture?'

I looked at him, not really believing what I'd heard. 'The one I brought back to you last week, the one you paid me in cash for.'

'Ah. I don't think I'm going to hang it.' He could see I was expecting some sort of explanation, and finally he gave me one. 'I'm not much of a bowerbird, as you've noticed. Would you like it?'

'Me? No. It's crap.'

'That's what you said Gill would say about it.'

'Well, I spent about fifteen hours looking at it, so I'm agreeing with her.' Stuart didn't seem at all put out by this. 'And what was the "particular reason" you wanted me to clean it?' He didn't answer at once, so I added, a bit sarcastically, 'Mr Henderson.'

'Ah, well, actually, so that I could meet you and ask you about Gillian and Oliver.'

'No-one recommended me?'

'No.'

'If you wanted to know about Gillian and Oliver, why

didn't you ask them yourself? Seeing as you're an old friend.'

'It's awkward. I wanted to know how they were. Really. Not how they said they were.' He could see I wasn't buying this for an explanation at all. 'OK. Gill and I used to be married.'

'Jesus.' I lit a cigarette straight away. 'Jesus.'

'Yes. Do you mind if I have one?'

'You don't smoke.'

'No, but I want one now.' He lit a Silk Cut, took a puff and looked at it in a slightly disappointed way, as if it wasn't any solution to the immediate problem.

'Jesus,' I repeated. 'Why did it . . . you know, go wrong?'

'Oliver.'

'Jesus.' I couldn't think of anything to say. 'Who knows?'

'Them. Me. Obviously. Mme Wyatt. You. A few people I haven't seen for years. My second wife. My second ex-wife. Not the girls. They don't know yet.'

'Jesus.'

He told me the story. He told it very straightforwardly, just the facts, as if he was reading from a newspaper. Not any old newspaper, either. Today's.

Oliver   My first pay packet, even if the second element in that substantive proved nugatory, there being no actual envelope. The 'wedge', as some of my fellow toilers refer to it, was merely thrust into my outstretched hand like that moment of divine contact in the Sistine Chapel. I knew my primal duty – the spirit of Roncesvalles still coursed within me – and hied my way to number 55. By the time I heard the soft-slipper shuffle of Mrs Dyer approaching the other side of the door, I was on one penitential knee. She looked at me with no immediate sign of cognition, re-, pre- or otherwise.

'Eleven twenty-five, Mrs D. Better late than never, as the Good Book has it.'

She took the money and – '*Etonne-moi!*' as Diaghilev said to Cocteau – started to count it. Then it disappeared out of sight into some crepuscular placket. Her parched and powdered lips slowly parted. Here came absolution for Ollie the Sinner, I thought.

'I want ten years' interest,' she said. 'Compound.' Then she shut the door.

Hey, isn't life full of gaudy surprises? Mrs D a major nickelfucker, think of that, eh? I hopscotched my way down her path like a sprite who's been at the margaritas.

She really must marry me, don't you think?

But I seem to be married already, don't I?

Gillian   One of the things I've always tried to teach the girls is that there's nothing particularly good or virtuous about wanting something. I don't put it like that, of course. In fact, I frequently don't put it at all. The best lessons children learn are those they learn for themselves.

It shocked me, the first time I saw close up – with Sophie – how much a child can want something. I'd noticed it before I had children, but only passingly. You know, you're in a shop, and there's usually a harassed mum with a couple of kids who are picking up things and saying, 'Want this', and the mum says, 'Put that down', or 'You can't have that today', or 'You've got enough crisps', or, just occasionally, 'All right, then, put it in the basket.' Such moments always struck me as rather primitive trials of strength, and I used to assume it was bad parenting that had let things get to this public stage. Well, that was priggish of me. Ignorant, as well.

Then I saw Sophie want things – in shops, in other people's houses, on television – with an intensity I simply couldn't remember from my own childhood. There was a stuffed owl belonging to the daughter of some friends. It wasn't rare or special in any way, just a felt owl glued to a perch like a parrot. She wanted that owl, she dreamed about it, she talked about it for months. She didn't want another one like it, she wanted *that one*; and the fact that it belonged to someone else, a friend too, didn't matter. She would have been a complete dictator if I'd let her dictate. Of course, Oliver would have allowed her anything.

I think children easily get into the habit of believing that just to say they want something is an interesting and valuable expression of their personality. I also think it's bad for them in later life: you want something, you get it. That's not what things are going to be like. How do you explain to a child that in later life it's normal to want something without ever standing a chance of getting it? Or the opposite: getting something only to find you didn't really want it after all, or that it wasn't what you thought it would be?

Marie   Want a cat.

Mme Wyatt   What do I desire? Well, since that I am an old woman – no, do not interrupt – since that I am an old woman, I have only what Stuart calls soft feelings. That was a good phrase, no? I want little comforts for myself. I do not want love or sex any more. I prefer a well-cut suit and a sole off the bone. I want a book written with a good style that does not have an unhappy ending. I want politeness and short conversations with friends for who I have respect. But in general I want things for others – for my daughter, for my granddaughters. I want the world to be not so menacing for them than it has been to me and the people I have known during my life. More and more, I want less and less. You see, I have only soft feelings.

Sophie   I want people in Africa to have enough to eat.

I want everyone to be a vegetarian and not eat animals.

I want to get married and have fifteen children. All right, six.

I want Spurs to win the League and the Cup and the European Cup and everything.

I want a new pair of trainers, but only when I've had enough wear out of these.

I want them to find a cure for cancer.

I want there not to be any more wars.

I want to do well in the exams and get into St Mary's.

I want Daddy to drive carefully and never get the glooms again.

I want Mummy to be more cheerful.

I want Marie to have a cat if Mummy thinks it's a good idea.

Terri   I want the kind of guy who turns out, when you get to know him better, to be exactly like how you took him to be when you first met him.

I want the kind of guy who calls when he says he'll call, and comes home when he says he'll come home.

I want the kind of guy who's happy being the kind of guy he is.

I want the kind of guy who wants the kind of woman I am.

That doesn't sound too much to ask, does it? Well, it's asking for the moon *and* the stars according to my friend Marcelle. I once asked her why so many of the men I'd been involved with didn't seem particularly well balanced, and she says, Terri, that's because all men are genetically related to stone crabs.

Gordon   Gordon here. That's right, Gordon Wyatt. As in, father of Gillian, and dastardly deserter of Marie-Christine. Don't get much of a look-in, do I? Knocking on a bit, of course, now. Got the old bus pass years ago. Bit of a scare in the grandfather clock department recently. Tick nearly didn't lead to tock, and the second Mrs W would have had to get out the crêpe. Not that anyone wears crêpe any more, do they? I must say, the way people dress for funerals and memorial services is pretty shocking. Even those who make an effort just look as if they're dressed for a job interview.

Oh, I know what people say. It's how you're feeling inside that counts, not how you're dressed outside. I'm sorry, but if you're crying bucketloads and looking as if you've stopped off on the way to a car-boot sale, that's not good enough for me. You're drawing attention to yourself in my book.

Sorry, that's a bit off tack. The second Mrs W would have pulled me up by now if she'd been around. Bit of a stickler about the general tendency to run off at the mouth.

I've been a lucky S.O.B., all things considered. I count my blessings. The children are doing well, three smashing grandchildren, pride of my life. Enough in the bank for the years ahead, fingers crossed.

It's not so much what I want as what I wish. I wish I could see Gillian again. Even a photo would be better than nothing. But the first Mrs W put up the Berlin Wall all those years ago, and the second has always been agin it. She says it's up to Gillian to get in touch if *she* wants to. Says I don't have the right to shove my way back into her life at this late stage. I do wonder what's become of her. She must be in her early forties by now. I don't even know if she's got kids. I don't even know if she's alive. That's an awful thought. No, I can comfort myself that if anything terrible had happened, I could count on Madame to track me down and twist the knife, just for old time's sake.

Look, you wouldn't by any chance have a photo of her on you? Sure? No, I suppose that would be breaking the rules. Anyway, that sounds like the door. Don't mention any of this, will you? The second Mrs W doesn't want to know, basically. And I do want a quiet time. I want that more than anything.

Mrs Dyer   I want the gate fixed. I want the doorbell fixed. I want that stupid monkey-puzzle tree chopped down, I've never liked it.

I want to join my husband. That's his ashes up there in the bedroom cupboard. I want to be scattered with him. I want us to fly away on the wind together.

Oliver
I want a hero: an uncommon want,
   When every year and month sends forth a new one,
Till, after cloying the gazettes with cant,
   The age discovers he is not the true one.

To want is to wish, and also to lack. So you wish for what you lack. Is it all as simple as that? Or can you want what you've already got? Indeed: you may desire the sultry continuance of what you already possess. And you can also want to be rid of what you have – in which case what you lack is the lack of something? Things do tend to overlap in this area, I find.

By the way, I don't want a hero. This is no time for

heroes. Even the names Roland and Oliver now sound like two tonsured veterans of the bowling green, right knees air-kissing the rubber mat as they curl their biased woods through the gentle evening sun towards the glinting jack. To be the hero of your own life is about as much as people can manage nowadays. To be a hero to others? No man is a hero to his valet, someone said. (Who? Some German sage, I would guess.) Then it's just as well I don't have a valet. If I did, he would turn out to be someone like Stuart. And I'd have to turn water into organic wine to get his vote.

For hero read that bland simulacrum the role model. No longer do you aspire to individualism, you aspire to category. The 'sporting hero' – a fetid and satirical contradiction in terms if ever I heard one – declares that he wishes to be a 'role model' for what he probably refers to as 'youngsters'. In other words: clones kindly apply. Whereas at the time of Roncesvalles, when Johnny Saracen's wickedly curved panga was slicing its way through the subcutaneous fat of Europe's soft underbelly ... *Momento* – haven't we been here before? Haven't *I* been here before?

I want to remember what I've told you previously. I wish I knew what my memory lacks. *Ha!*

Ellie   I said, probably earlier than I needed to, 'Do you have a condom with you?'

He looked a bit surprised. 'No. I can pop out and get some.'

I said, 'Look, just so we know where we are, I always insist on condoms.'

Some boys get pissed off at that. So it's a sort of test, too.

He just said, 'Well, that works both ways.'

'How do you mean?'

'I mean neither of us has to worry. About anything.'

That was a nice thing to say. I think, anyway.

When he got to the door, he turned. 'Anything else you want? Shampoo? Toothbrush? Dental tape?'

Stuart's much more fun than he looks, you know.

Mme Wyatt   So, I have convinced you, with my little discourse about soft feelings, about not desiring things, wanting them only for others? Let me explain you this. The old are very good at being old, it is a skill they learn. They know what you are expecting from them and they give it to you. What do I desire? I desire, bitterly and without cease, to be young again. I detest my old age more than I detested anything in my youngness. I desire love. I desire to be loved. I desire sex. I desire to be held and to be caressed. I desire to fuck. I desire not to die. I also desire to die in my sleep, suddenly, not to die like my mother, screaming with the cancer, doctors unable to control the pain, until they decide to give her morphine to kill her, then she is silent. I desire my daughter to know that I am more different from her than she can possibly know, that I love her always but do not always like her so much. I also desire that my husband, who betrayed me, suffer because of it. Sometimes I go to church and pray. I am not a believer, but I pray that there is a God and that in another life my husband be punished as a sinner. I want him to burn in the hell I do not believe in.

So you see, I also have hard feelings. You are very naïve about us, the old people.

13 : Sofa Legs

Oliver   Stuart has a Theory, and I leave you to reflect for a few jocund nano-seconds on the inapt conjoining – the miscegenation – of the first and fourth words of this sentence.

Stuart believes that farm animals should be allowed to go for walkies and sleep in the best b-and-b accommodation. Fino by me. Stuart believes that vegetables shouldn't be as bulgy with drugs as a Tour de France cyclist. Amontillado by me. Stuart believes that the noble orbs of the downy veal calf should not be afflicted, during their terminal blink at this sad world of ours, by the peripheral awareness of a lumpenslaughterer wielding a chainsaw. Oloroso by me.

Stuart, lulled by the popular applause such virtuous

sentiments provoke, allows himself to speculate further. An Englishman equipped with a theory, oh dear: it's like wearing a tweed suit at Cap d'Agde. Don't do it, Stuart! 'But no, they will not; they must still/ Wrest their neighbour to their will.' So Stuart, in six-ply Jaeger from hoof to plume, dog-paddles among the nudists with the following proposition clenched between his canines: that humankind itself should become organic; that cityfolk may claim kinship with the stressful porker; that we must snort the pure and addictive air far away from those dread acronyms of pollution he thrills to scare us with; that we should crop the fruits of the hedgerow and o'ercome the suppertime bunny with simple bow and arrow, then trip an Arcadian measure on the humectant moss as in a sentimental vision by Claude Le Lorrain.

In other words, he wants the human race to become hunter-gatherers again! But the whole point, O Stuartus Rusticus, is that this is the very state we have spent so many millennia fleeing. Nomads aren't nomads because they *like* being nomads, but because they have no choice. And now that our modern age has given them the choice, see what they nobly prefer: the off-road vehicle, the automatic rifle, telly and a bottle of hooch. Just like us! And one further point is that if we were to display in some instructional diorama representative samples of organic versus industri-ally-farmed man, which of the two might be the most plausibly represented by my newly slimline chum? So his theory, apart from being demonstrably absurd, is, to use a less technical phrase, a bit fucking rich coming from him.

147

Stuart   It's not that I expect gratitude. It's just that I think contempt is out of order.

So I told him.

He came into my office for his money. It would be easier for Joan, who's my assistant, to pay him, as she's in charge of wages; but for some reason Oliver insists on coming to me direct. Well, that's fine. He also says things like, 'Come for my wedge Mr Boss-Man, *sir*', which are either meant to be funny or to be how the other drivers talk. Which they don't, of course: normal people put their heads round Joan's door and say, 'Is this a good time?' or 'Am I a bit early?' But that's fine too.

It's a bit less fine that Oliver likes to throw himself down in a chair and chew the cud while I have a business to run.

It's a bit less fine that there's a large dent in the nearside front wing of Oliver's van, which he didn't report because he claims not to know how it got there.

It's a bit less fine that Oliver likes to leave my door open so that Joan can hear him treat me with what he probably thinks of as familiarity, but which might strike an outsider as something else. He isn't popular around the office, by the way. That's why I've started sending him on longer trips.

So he sat there, with the van keys hooked over his thumb and dangling into his palm. Then he started counting his money very slowly, as if I was the most untrustworthy employer in London. Finally, he looked up and said, 'No deductions for putting up Gill's shelves, eh?' And he gave me a stupid wink.

Perhaps I mentioned that I've been doing a bit of DIY round at their house. Well, how else would it get done?

148

I got up and shut the door. Then I went and stood behind my desk. 'Look, Oliver, can we just agree, work's work, OK?'

I said it quite reasonably and reached for the phone. As I was dialling, his arm came across the desk and cut off the line. 'Work's work, is it?' he said in his silly, sneering voice, and then began some stupid rant about whether *a* is always *a* and couldn't it sometimes be *b*. You know the sort of thing. Pure wankery dressed up as philosophy. And all the time he was clenching and unclenching his fist over the keys, and I think it was this that finally made me lose my patience somewhat.

'Look, Oliver, I've work to do, so –'

'So just fuck off, eh?'

'Yes, that's the long and the short of it, just fuck off, OK?'

He stood up, facing me, still closing and opening his right hand – keys, no keys, keys, no keys – like some cheap magician on the telly. At the same time, he looked as if he was trying to be menacing, which made it worse. Sillier, too. I wasn't in the least afraid. But I was extremely cross.

'You're not in the middle of a French village now,' I said.

Well, that took the wind from his sails. Collapse of stout party indeed. He got all white and sweaty. 'She told you,' he said. '*She* told you. The –'

I wasn't going to have him insulting Gillian, so I jumped in first. 'She didn't tell me. I was there.'

'Oh yes, you and who else?' which apart from being a stupid question made him sound as if he was back in the playground at school.

'No-one else. Just me. I saw it all. Now fuck off, Oliver.'

Oliver   Impossible not to cop, *de temps en temps*, the crucial verity that the accumulated wisdom of the ages and the masses, whether expressed in the form of the bum-numbing folk tale, the preposterously anthropomorphic animal fable, or the mercifully brief cracker motto, is, not to put too fine a point on it, generally a few candles short of a bedside light. Rub two clichés together and you could not ignite an *idée reçue*. Bind a dozen anthologisable apothegms into a faggot and you would not get much kindling.

Concentrate, Ollie, concentrate. To the present instance, *please*.

Well, if you insist. The present instance expressing itself in a most peculiar if popular moral injunction, namely: don't shoot the messenger. Why the eff you see kay not is what I say. That's what messengers are for. And don't give me that line about it not being the messenger's fault. It *is* his fault: he spoilt your day, why shouldn't he pay for it? Besides, messengers are two a penny. If they weren't, they'd be generals or politicians.

Did she know? That, we have to assert, is the question of questions. I admit that, ten years ago, I laid public hands on the fair Gillian, not a hair of whose head has since been touched. The circumstances, you will recall, were most provoking. *She* had been most provoking, for a goodly time – she, whose technique of crowd control (there being such a tumult of characters making up the unified field you know by the simple name of Oliver) is usually so subtle. Gillian is a devotee of the softly-softly approach to domestic policing. On this occasion not; and on this occasion, prodded and bodkined and poniarded as never before or since, I struck her. Handing over hectares of moral high ground, apart from anything else. And Stuart was watching, from some crepuscular inglenook or rancid wankpit whose location he failed to reveal to me.

That question again: did she know? We hear the echo of each other's laughter, do we not? It is true that the scientific odds against human life developing in the universe, against the necessary conjunction of quasars and pulsars and Johnny Quarks and amoebic spunk or whatever – my physics has always been a bit approximate – is several billion trillion to one (my mathematics too, for that matter). But your savvy local bookmaker would probably offer you about the same odds against Stuart managing to locate himself in a distant Languedocian village, hitherto unknown to him, at the very precise moment in the history of the aforesaid universe when Ollie was being goaded into his sole and much regretted act of domestic violence.

So she planned it. And she planned it all for him. She acted out that lie, and all its preparations, and she's let me live with it ever since.

Truth will out, old bean, eh? Aha, I hear you yelp, Ollie at the point of crisis falls back on just the very accumulated wisdom of the populace he affects to despise. Well, wrong again, fartface. The point is, as historians, philosophers, brute politicians and everyone else with a head halfway screwed on concurs, truth mostly does not out. It mostly ins, until the day it is interred in our bones. That's the grim norm. But in the present very rare instance, and drawing no wider conclusions from it, truth did indeed . . .

The See You En Tee.

Gillian   Stuart's been putting up shelves. Marie really seems to have taken to him. When he uses the drill she puts her hands over her ears and squeals. Stuart gets her to hand him screws and rawlplugs and things, and puts them in the corners of his mouth if he's got his hands full. He turns round to her, four screws between his lips, and she smiles back at him.

Mme Wyatt   I dialled the house. Sophie answered.

'Hello, Grand'mère,' she said. 'Do you want to speak to Stuart?'

'Why should I want to speak to Stuart?' I ask.

'He's putting up shelves.'

I know she is only a child, but even so I did not think it was the most logical answer I have ever heard. Perhaps it is the result of the English education. A French child will certainly understand the significance of the word *why*.

'Sophie, I have all the shelves I need.' Well, they will never understand logic unless someone demonstrates it to them, will they?

There was a silence. I could hear that she was trying to think for herself. 'Mummy's out and Daddy's digging up carrots in Lincolnshire.'

'Tell your mother to call me when she returns.'

Really. You English.

Stuart   I suddenly saw what they meant about wallpaper. Not the actual wallpaper – in fact, the last tenants painted all over the top of it, so that the whole place is white except for the yellow bits of Sellotape where they took their posters down.

No, I was in the kitchen making supper – nothing complicated, just a mushroom risotto (I've got this chap who goes out to Epping Forest at dawn and we have what he finds in the shops by mid-morning). Sophie was doing her homework at the table, Marie was 'helping' as we like to call it, and I was just ladling in some more stock when out of the corner of my eye I saw the leg of the sofa. Actually, 'leg' is a bit of an exaggeration. 'Foot' isn't quite right either. It's more a sort of wooden sphere, really, which would probably have taken a castor originally, but –

What? Oh, Gill was up in the studio. She's been very pressed with a commission they wanted back sooner than they'd said.

– and of course it had been secondhand when we bought it. Our first sofa, which I used to call a settee until corrected. Not that I minded – being corrected, I mean. Gill made new covers for it, a jolly yellow fabric I remember. Now it's dark blue, and even more battered, and there are kids' things all over it, but the foot or whatever you bloody well want to call it is still there, just there in the corner of my eye . . .

What? Oh, Oliver was up in Lincolnshire still. Carrots, cabbages, things he can't go wrong with. What do I do about Oliver? Send him to Morocco for some lemons?

We used to watch television together on it.

'Ticky,' says Marie, and my attention is drawn back.

'Thank you, Marie,' I say, 'that was very helpful.' It was sticking and needed a good stir and scrape.

We used to watch television together on it. When we were first married. Not that we were anything except 'first' married, when you look at it in the cold light of day. We had a television which was such an antique it didn't have remote control. And we had a rule that whoever wanted to change channel – as long as the other one agreed – had to get up and punch the button. I'd just get up and reach across and do it. But Gill would sort of flow off the sofa, onto her front, and lie there reaching up to the box's controls. She wore grey stone-washed 501s with trainers and green socks. I don't mean she only had green socks, just that she always did in my memory. Normally, when she'd changed the channel, she'd go into reverse gear, backwards on her knees and then up onto the sofa again. But sometimes, just occasionally, she'd lie there looking up at the screen, and then turn and glance back at me from the floor, with the light from the television playing on her face . . . That's one of the ways I've always remembered her.

'Ticky,' says Marie.

'Yes,' I reply. '*Very* ticky.'

The phone number. That's another thing. It's just a collection of digits, after all. And it's acquired an 020 8-prefix since we lived here. But those last seven numbers, they're still the same, exactly the same. Who'd have thought it? That a set of numbers can cause pain. Such pain. Every time.

Terri   My friends who live on the bay have a trap for catching their own crabs. They bait it with fish heads and sling it into the water on a rope from the little pier at the end of their yard. They pulled it up to show me. There were these half-dozen crabs in it, all this incredible silky-blue color. And someone asked: how can you tell if they're male or female? Someone else made a joke as you'd expect, but Bill said, 'These are all male.' Females have pink claws, apparently. Someone said: hey, blue for a boy and pink for a girl, but I was intrigued.

'Why are there only males in the trap?' I ask.

'That's normal,' Bill tells me. 'The females are too smart to get caught.'

We all laugh, but as my friend Marcelle says: remind you of something?

Oliver   A thought, a veritable thought, which came to me as I was plodding south to Stamford with my cornucopia of carrots and my booty of brassica.

You've noticed – how can you not have? – that Stuart has become a swank. No, worse – because even less convincing – a positive swell. The suits which bespeak of bespoke, the BMW, the exercise programme, the fascistic haircut, the opinions on matters social, political and economic, the blithe assumption that he represents the norm, the Croesal disbursement of moidores and doubloons – the fucking money, in other words, and all that flows from it. The fucking money.

My question is merely this: does our impresario imagine he is staging *The Revenge of the Tortoise*? That end-of-the-pier playlet, *The Parable of the Outdistanced One*? Is that why he primps and preens and swanks and swells? Because he thinks that he has in some way *won*? If so, let me tell you – and him – this: I have in my time investigated the voluminous myth-kitty which our spavined species has assembled down the millennia for its comfort and edification, and I have a word of advice for those who cannot reach the end of the day's winding path without a toke of myth. My counsel is this and thus: dream on. The pig did not fly; the stone rebounded from the helmet of Goliath, who promptly ate David for breakfast; the fox easily acquired the grapes by cutting down the vine with a power saw; and Jesus resideth not with his Father.

As I swooped down the sliproad to mingle with the credulous on the motorway, I decided to idle away the dull furlongs with literary genre. Are you sitting comfortably?

Realism: Hare runs faster than Tortoise. Much faster. And is smarter. Therefore wins. By a long way. OK?

Sentimental Romanticism: Complacent Hare snoozes by side of road while morally worthy Tortoise trundles past to winning line.

Surrealism (or Advertising): Tortoise, equipped with rollerblades, neat black-leather backpack and shades, glides effortlessly ahead while outpaced leveret cacks his scut.

The Collected Letters: Dear Furry, Why don't you 'hare' on ahead and wait for me by the hedge? I'll be there as soon as I can slip away. You don't think they're on to us, do you? Your own 'Shelley'.

PC Kids' Story (written by ex-hippie): Hare and Tortoise, having seen through the social and political structures which incite public displays of competitiveness, abandon their race and live peacefully in a yurt, refusing all media requests for interviews.

Limerick: There was an old Tortoise called Stu/ Who concurred with what limericks do/ Which is comfort and coddle/ The plain-thinking noddle/ Of the stupidest beasts in the zoo.

Post-modernism: I, the author, made up this story. It's a mere construct. The Hare and the Tortoise don't actually 'exist', you realise that, I hope?

And so on. Now can you see what's wrong with our impresario's cockle-warming mythette, *The Revenge of the Tortoise*? What's wrong is this: *it never happens*. The world, being constructed as it is, will not allow it. Realism is our given, our only mode, *triste* truth as it might be to some.

14: Love, etc

Gillian   Each morning, as the girls set off for school, I kiss them and say, 'I love you.' I say it because it's true, because they should hear it and know it. I also say it for its magical powers, for its ability to ward off the world.

When did I last say it to Oliver? I can't remember. After a few years, we got into the habit of dropping the 'I'. One of us would say, 'Love you,' and the other would say, 'Love you too.' There's nothing shocking about that, nothing out of the ordinary, but one day I caught myself wondering if it wasn't significant. As if you weren't taking responsibility for the feeling any more. As if it had become somehow more general, less focused.

Well, I suppose that's the answer, isn't it? It's my children who bring out the 'I' in the 'I love you.' Do 'I' still love

Oliver? Yes, 'I' think so, 'I' suppose so. You could say I'm managing love.

You organise a marriage, you protect your children, you manage love, you run your life. And sometimes you stop and wonder if that's true at all. Do you run your life, or does your life run you?

Stuart   I've come to some conclusions in my time. I'm a grown-up person, I've been an adult longer than I've been a child and an adolescent. I've looked at the world. My conclusions may not be blindingly original, but they're still mine.

For instance, I'm suspicious of people comparing things with other things. In the days when I was more impressed with Oliver, I used to think that this mania of his proved he had not just better powers of description than I had, but also a better understanding of the world. The memory is like a left-luggage office. Love is like the free market. So-and-so is behaving just like some character you've never heard of in some opera you've never heard of. Now I think all these fancy comparisons were a way of not looking at the original object, of not looking at the world. They were just distractions. And this is why Oliver hasn't changed – developed – grown up – call it what you will. Because it's only by looking at the world out there as it is and the world in here as it is that you grow up.

I don't mean that you like what you find, or that what you find is what you want. Usually, it isn't. But Oliver just makes pretty patterns in the air like –

You see how tempting it is? I was going to say like a firework or something. And you might have thought: oh, that's right, but you'd be thinking about the firework and I bet that's what you'd remember rather than Oliver himself. And if it was Oliver doing the comparison, everyone would be different kinds of firework – Oh, Stuart, old Stuart, he's a bit of a damp squib, ho ho – and it would all be very entertaining and very . . . wrong.

I said that what you find isn't necessarily what you want. Let's take love. It isn't like we thought it would be beforehand. Can we all agree on that? Better, worse, longer, shorter, overrated, underrated, but not the same. Also, different for different people. But that's something you only learn slowly: what love is like for you. How much of it you've got. What you'll give up for it. How it lives. How it dies. Oliver used to have a theory he called *Love, etc*: in other words, the world divides into people for whom love is everything and the rest of life is a mere 'etc', and people who don't value love enough and find the most exciting part of life is the 'etc'. It was the sort of line he was peddling when he stole my wife and I suspected it was bollocks at the time, and now I know it's absolute bollocks not to mention boastful bollocks. People don't divide up that way.

And another thing. Beforehand, you think: when I grow up I'll love someone, and I hope it goes right, but if it goes wrong I'll love another person, and if that goes wrong I'll love another person. Always assuming that you can find these people in the first place and that they'll let you love them. What you expect is that love, or the ability to love, is always there, waiting. I was going to say, waiting with the engine running. You see the temptation of Oliver-speak? But I don't think that love – and life – are like that. You can't make yourself love someone, and you can't, in my experience, make yourself stop loving someone. In fact, if you want to divide people up in the matter of love, I'd suggest doing it this way: some people are fortunate, or unfortunate, enough to love several people, either one after the other, or overlapping; while other people are fortunate, or unfortunate, enough to be able to love only once in their life. They love once and, whatever happens, it doesn't go away. Some people can only do it once. I've come to realise that I'm one of these.

All of which may be bad news for Gillian.

Oliver 'Life is first boredom, then fear'? No, I think not, except for the emotionally constipated.

Life is first comedy, then tragedy? No, the genres swirl like paint in a centrifuge.

Life is first comedy, then farce?

Life is first tipsiness, then addiction and hangover at the same time?

Life is first soft drugs, then hard? Soft porn, then hard? Soft-centred chocolates, then hard?

Life is first the scent of wild flowers, then of toilet freshener?

The poet has it that the three events of life are 'birth, copulation and death', a bleak wisdom which thrilled my adolescence. Later, I realised Old Possum had omitted some of the other central moments: the first cigarette, snow on a tree in blossom, Venice, the joy of shopping, flight in all its senses, fugue in all its senses, that moment when you change gear at high speed and your passenger's beloved head does not even stir on its spinal column, *risotto nero*, the third-act trio from *Rosenkavalier*, the chuckle of a child, that second cigarette, a longed-for face coming into focus at airport or railway station . . .

Or, to be argumentative rather than decorative, why did the poet list copulation rather than love? Maybe Old P was more of a goer than I thought – I am no student of biography – but imagine yourself on your deathbed, reflecting on that brief allotted time between an arrival of which you were not conscious and a departure on which you will be unavailable for comment: would you be deluding yourself or speaking true if you maintained that the chief events of your life had been to do with the breathless unfolding of the heart, rather than with a catalogue of shaggings, even if they numbered *mille tre*?

The world is full of vile things. Agreed? And I'm not just referring to toilet freshener, vile, viler than any bog-pong as it is. Let me quote you what I quoted you once before. 'It's the vileness that ruins love. And the laws, and properties, and financial worries and the police state. If conditions had been different, love would have been different.' Agreed? I am not proposing that the genial London bobby, so helpful to the disoriented tourist, is much of an immediate menace to *l'amore*. But in general terms, agreed? Love in a leafy democratic suburb on six figures a year is different from love in a Stalinist prison camp.

Love, etc. That has always been my formula, my theory,

my wisdom. I knew it at once, as an infant knows its mother's smile, as a fledged duckling takes to the water, as a fuse burns towards a bomb. I always knew. I got there earlier – half a lifetime earlier – than some I could mention.

'Financial worries'. Yes, they do drag one down, don't they? I leave that side of things to Gillian, but I have had my moments of pecuniary *inquiétude*. Do you think the local police state, benign version, should give out love grants? There's family benefit, there are funeral grants, so why not some state allowance for lovers? Isn't the state there to facilitate the pursuit of happiness? Which in my book is just as important as life or liberty. Just as important, I realise, because synonymous. Love is my life and it is my liberty.

Another argument, one for the bureaucrats. Happy people are healthier than unhappy people. Make people happier and you reduce the burden on the National Health Service. Imagine the news headlines: NURSES SENT HOME ON FULL PAY OWING TO OUTBREAK OF HAPPINESS. Oh, I know there are certain instances where illness strikes regardless. But don't quibble, just dream along.

You're not expecting me to refer to individual cases, are you? Or rather, the individual case of Mr and Mrs Oliver Russell. Not that we are such. Mr Oliver Russell and Ms Gillian Wyatt, as the pustular postman, lubricious hotel clerk and nickle-fucking tax-collector see us. You don't want me to go into *detail*, do you? That would be Stuart-like behaviour. Someone around here must represent both the ludic and the abstract. Someone around here must be allowed to soar a little. Stuart could only *soar* in a microlite, chugging along like a motor-mower in the empyrean.

Another reason for not going into detail is recent events. Recent discoveries. I really *am* trying not to think about them.

Mme Wyatt   Love and marriage. The Anglo-Saxons have always believed that they themselves marry for love, while the French marry for children, for family, for social position, for business. No, wait a minute, I am merely repeating what one of your own experts has written. She – it was a woman – divided her life between the two worlds, and she was observing, not judging, not at first. She said that for the Anglo-Saxons marriage was founded on love, which was an absurdity since love is anarchic and passion is sure to die, and that this was no sound basis for marriage. On the other hand, she said, we French marry for sensible, rational reasons of family and property, because unlike you we recognise the necessary fact that love cannot be contained within the structure of marriage. Therefore we have made sure that it exists only outside of it. This, of course, is not perfect either, in fact in some ways it is equally absurd. But perhaps it is a more rational absurdity. Neither solution is ideal and neither can be expected to lead to happiness. She was a wise woman, this expert of yours, and therefore a pessimist.

I do not know why Stuart chose to tell you all those years ago that I was having an affair. I told him in confidence and he acted like the popular press in your country. Well, it was a difficult time for him, with his marriage breaking up, so perhaps I forgive him.

But since you know, I will inform you a little about it. He – Alan – was English, he was married, we were both in our . . . no, that is my secret. He had been married for . . . well, for many years. At first it was about sex. You are shocked? It always is, whatever anyone says. Oh, it is about an end to loneliness, and interests to share, and talking, talking, but it is really about sex. He said that after so many years making love to his wife, it had become like driving along a familiar stretch of motorway, you knew all the curves and the signs so well. I did not find this comparison exactly *galant*. But we had agreed – as lovers habitually do, with a kind of arrogant naïveté – only to speak the truth to one another. After all, there were so many lies to be told every time, simply so that we could meet. And I had set the example. I told him that I did not intend to marry again and I did not intend to live with another man. This did not mean that I was not going to fall in love again, but – well, I have explained that. Indeed, I was beginning to love him at the time of the . . . incident.

He had arrived for the weekend. He lived about twenty miles away. I had been busy that week and so, when he came, I said we must go shopping for what we need. We drove to the Waitrose, we parked the car, we got the *chariot* – the trolley – we talked about what I would cook, we filled the trolley, I put in various things I needed for when he wasn't there, I paid with my Waitrose card. By the time we got into the car again I saw he was in a sudden depression. I did not ask, not at first, I waited to see what he would do – after all, it was his depression, not mine. And he was heroic, because he was also beginning to love me, and that is when heroism is possible. I mean, the heroism to fight your own character.

We passed a happy weekend together and at the end of it I asked him why he had suddenly become depressed in the supermarket. And his face became sombre all over again, and he said, 'My wife pays with a Waitrose card as well.' At that moment, I saw it all and I knew that the relationship was without hope. It was not just the card, of course, it was the carpark, the trolley, the Friday night shoppers filling the store, it was the fact, the terrible fact that your new mistress also needs rolls of kitchen towel just so much as your wife. He had walked along the same aisles, even if they were twenty miles separated. And it probably made him think that before very long, with me, he would be driving along that too familiar stretch of motorway.

I did not blame him. We just thought differently about love. I was able to enjoy the day, the weekend, the sudden time. I knew that love was fragile, volatile, *fugace*, anarchic, so I would allow love its entire space, its empire. He knew, or at least he could not persuade himself from thinking, that love was not a magical state, or not one only, but rather the start of a journey, which led, sooner or later, to a Waitrose card. That was the only way he could think, despite me telling him that I did not want to live with anyone again, or marry. So, fortunately, in a way, he had found out sooner rather than later.

He went back to his wife. And – I do not say this because I want to pretend to virtue – he may even have been happier when he went back. He had learned the lesson of the kitchen towel. What do you think? Nowadays La Fontaine's Fables take place in the supermarket.

Mrs Dyer   What's that? Speak up. I'm Labour, is that what you want to know? Always have been. My husband too, when he was alive. Forty years, never a cross word. I'm ready to join him. Are you selling something? I don't want anything. I'm not letting you in. I've read about people like you in the paper. That's why I had the meters put on the outside wall. So be off with you, whatever it is you want. I'm shutting the door now. I'm Labour, if that's what you want to know. But you'll have to send a car if you want my vote. It's my legs. Right, I'm shutting the door now. Whatever it is, I don't want it. Thank you.

Terri   You know how, you're falling in love, everything seems, like, totally original? The words they use, the way they hold you in bed, the way they drive a car? You think, I've never been talked to, or made love to, or driven, like this before. And you have, of course, most likely. Unless you're twelve or something. It's just that you've never noticed before, or you've forgotten. And then if there's something you really haven't heard or done before, however small, then it seems, well, so original you could scream, and such a part of how you are together.

Like, I had this Mickey Mouse watch – I know it sounds ... I don't know what – anyway, I did. Never wore it to work, because what would you think if the maitresse D at a

French restaurant wore a Mickey Mouse watch? You'd think we got Pluto in the kitchen making jello or something, right? So I kept the watch at home, by the bed, and wore it only on Sundays when we were closed. And when Stuart moved in with me one of the first things I noticed was he always knew exactly which day of the week it was when he woke up, even if he was half asleep. And I knew he knew it was Sunday because when he stirred and put his arm across me and burrowed into the back of me, he'd ask, 'What does Mickey say it is?' And I'd look, and I'd go, 'Mickey says it's twenty of nine,' or whatever.

Does that embarrass you? It still makes me almost want to cry, just thinking of it. And because he was a Brit, there were all kinds of little phrases he used that I didn't know and they seemed, like I say, totally original. And part of him. And part of us. He'd say 'Bob's your uncle', and 'I'm only here for the beer', and 'The proof of the pudding is in the eating.'

The first time he said that, I thought he was talking about the restaurant. About some dessert that hadn't panned out. And it's kind of a weird phrase when you think about it because the only way you can really tell if a dessert is any good is by eating it, same as prime rib or an oyster stew. So it's not just a cliché, it's so obvious that it's not even worth saying. But by the time I thought about it, it was too late, the phrase was there, already part of us, and the fact that we ran a restaurant made it a private joke. 'P of the P,' Stuart would whisper to me, when we were with other people.

Well, P of the P to you, ex-husband, P of the fucking P to you. I've been out with a number of guys, and I'm currently in a relationship, so I'm not just talking about you, Stuart Hughes, but if you take this personally I'll understand. Some people lie when they fall in love, some people tell the truth. Some people do both, by telling honest lies, which is what most of us do. 'Yes, I like jazz,' we'll say, when we mean, 'I could like it with you.' Love is meant to change your life — right? So it's an honest lie if you say things you aren't sure of. All the way up to 'I want you to have my kids.'

And that's all the way it went up to in your case, didn't it, Stuart? Proof of the fucking Pud to you, Mr. Ex. Show the photograph, that's what I say, show the photograph. Some lies are more honest than others.

Ellie   Look, I'm not complaining, but if you really want to know it goes like this.

I'm twenty-three, nearly twenty-four, and I've been what those surveys call sexually active for a third of my life. Yeah, yeah, fifteen, I know, against the law or whatever. Also normal. And if I counted – which I don't – I bet I've shagged far more boys than my mum has in her entire life, and that's the way it is too. And I've lived with one of them so I've been in love. And I've had a married man for a bit, which was OK but not much different except he told me more lies than the others. And – what else? – I've been to college and I've got a job and I've been round the world and I've done the usual drugs and I've got the vote and I dress how I want and people who haven't seen me for a year or so or more say, Hey, Ellie, you're really so *grown up* now.

Except I don't feel it. Not when I look at people who are grown up, people like Gillian, say. Then I feel incredibly young, and a fraud if you really want to know, as if someone's going to point the finger any moment and say I'm ignorant and a fake and I have the mental and emotional age of twelve, and I know I'll just agree. I can't imagine I'll ever pass for grown up.

When I said that about the married man I didn't mean Stuart. I mean, I hadn't counted him.

On the other hand, when you look at them, most grown-ups are really fuck-ups. My parents split up when I was ten. At least half my friends' parents split up too. They always say: oh Ellie, it's not a failure, you mustn't think of it like that, blah blah, it's just that we grew apart and we're being so much more honest than *our* parents, who carried on living together even when they were bored to death and hated one another, just because of social convention, so can't you see that it's both more honest and in the long run less painful blah blah blah when all they're really saying is I'm shagging someone else.

Or look at this lot. There's Gillian and Oliver and I don't think much of that marriage. There's Stuart: two marriages adding up to a total of what, five and a bit years between them? Even old Mme Wyatt – she ended up on her own.

People make mistakes. Sure, I agree. It's just that when I look at people older than me they've either split up or they're in relationships I wouldn't want to be in myself. Yes, I am judgemental, since you ask. When you see experts and people in the law and people on TV saying, 'We must take the concept of fault out of the breakdown of relationships,' I think: oh no we shouldn't, what we should do is put it back in. Everyone's at fault so no-one's at fault, that's what they think, don't they? Well, not me, not me.

What I want to know is this. Most of the grown-ups I know seem to be fuck-ups, one way or another. So is that the way you get to be grown up, by fucking up? In that case I don't think I'll bother.

P.S. About Gillian. Of course I admire her. She's very good at her work, and she runs her life in a way I never could. And I like her too. It's just that . . . look, when we're in the studio and someone brings in a picture she's very smart at spotting fakes.

So what's she doing with Oliver?

Stuart   First love is the only love.

Oliver   As much love as possible is the only love.

Gillian   True love is the only love.

Stuart   I don't mean you can't love again. Some people can, even if some people can't. But whether you can or can't, first love can never be repeated. And whether you can or can't, first love never lets you go. Second love lets you go. First, never.

Oliver   Misprise me not. 'Twas not the catechism of Casanova, the justification of Giovanni. Sexual Stakhanovism is for those with no imagination. I meant, if anything, the contrary. We need as much love as possible because there is so little of it to go round, don't you find?

Gillian   True love is solid love, day-to-day love, reliable love, love that never lets you down. You think that sounds boring? I don't. I think it sounds deeply romantic.

Stuart   P.S. By the way, and incidentally, who ever said that love makes us better people, or makes us behave better? Who ever said that?

Stuart   P.P.S. I'd like to make another point because nobody else has done so. Someone said that being in love makes you liable to fall in love. I'd just like to say: not half as much as *not* being in love does.

Stuart   P.P.P.S. And another thing. Love leads to happiness. That's what everyone believes, isn't it? That's what I used to believe, too, all those years ago. I don't any more.

You look surprised. Think about it. Examine your own life. Love leads to happiness? Come off it.

15 : Do You Know
What's Up?

Terri   You see, Stuart and I got on well enough. We fought about a few things, like vacations – he never wanted to take one and when we did he wasn't any good at doing nothing. I've never seen anyone so miserable as Stuart on a beach. But he was a generous man, had fun buying me things, we lived well, we had friends who came over. We could've stayed married – for Christ's sake, people in way worse shape than us stay married and don't think anything's wrong.

I guess we'd agree it started to unravel the day we spent those eighteen minutes at the therapist. But we'd disagree about the why. And we aren't going to any therapist to work through *that* disagreement. We didn't have to work through it for the court either. We both wanted a divorce, there were no kids, Stuart was generous, like I said. Why bother distributing the truth as well as the property? So it just lies there, this disagreement of ours, this disagreement about the truth. Lies there like a piece of junk on the ocean floor. You know – you're out swimming, it's a beautiful day, the water's clear, you're happy, and all you can see is this pile of rusting junk on the bottom. Home for a bunch of crabs. That's all you can see.

Stuart   Terri? You're still asking me about Terri? Look, that stuff's all in the past for me, it's over and done with. Tell you what: I'll just put my case on the record and leave it at that. If you don't believe me, that's OK. What I mean is: my account is non-negotiable.

OK, so we moved in together, we married, Terri didn't want children at first, but that was fine. We got on, we had fun, we jogged along. Then . . . well, put it this way. Terri for some reason became obsessed with Gillian. She also decided at about this time – and she made it quite clear to me – that she didn't ever want to have children with me. And what can you do about that? If either of us needed a therapist, it was her. But the problem was insurmountable. So it could never be what I would regard as a full marriage. So we separated. Later, we divorced. It was painful, but we wanted different things out of the marriage, and once you recognise that, then it's time to call it a day, isn't it? End of story.

Terri   'My account is non-negotiable.' He actually *said* that? Is it just me, am I over-sensitive, or does that feel like ten below zero? Business terms may be non-negotiable, Stuart, American foreign policy may be non-negotiable, Stuart, but we're talking human relations here, or hadn't you noticed?

Fact. Stuart was deeply trashed by his first wife. He was damaged, he was hurting in ways he didn't know he could hurt. She really put him through it, leaving him in the dirt and going off with his best friend. It took Stuart a long time to learn to trust again. Fact. He did learn to trust again, with me. Fact. Just because you've been trashed by someone, it doesn't mean you stop thinking about them. Usually the reverse. As in, becoming obsessed by them. Fact. Stuart had mentioned kids when we were first together, I said I wasn't ready, he said that was fine, we had all the time in the world. Fact. Stuart didn't mention kids again until the week after our aborted visit to the therapist.

Now, this next part is not a fact, but it is my considered opinion, which I suddenly came to one day, and everything in me confirmed it – every instinct, every part of my brain, every moment of observation, every way of looking into the past. You recall what I was saying about the honest lies you tell at the start of a relationship? And the one Stuart told, the big one, was 'I want you to have my kids.' You know why it was a lie? Because the truth, which took me three years of marriage to figure out, was this. What Stuart wanted, what he wanted me to have, wasn't my kids but Gillian's. Don't you see?

Hey, Stuart, now that *is* non-negotiable.

Gillian   Do you know what's up with Oliver?

He came back from Lincolnshire in a really foul mood. Sophie ran to the door, and the next thing I heard was Oliver stomping upstairs. Sophie came back and said, 'Daddy's in a grump.'

People's moods. How do you deal with them? I'm not a therapist and I wouldn't be any good as one anyway. So all I can do is what I always do: I carry on as normal, I remain as cheerful as possible, and if Oliver doesn't want to pick up on my mood, then I'm sorry but he can get on with his own. I'm not – what's that awful word? – confrontational. I ask and I listen if and as required. I'm here if he needs me. On the other hand, I'm not a nursemaid and I'm not a mother – except to my own children.

When he came down I asked how his day had been.

'Carrots. Leeks. Ducks.'

I asked about the traffic.

'The highway was replete with poltroons, dupes and deceivers.'

So I gave normality a final try. I took him to see the shelves Stuart had put up. He looked at them for a long time – peering from close up, standing back as if he was in the National Gallery, knocking on the wood with his knuckles, contorting himself to see how they were fixed to the wall, playing with a spirit level Stuart had left behind. It was a typical performance, if more over the top than usual.

'They're not painted,' I said, to fill the silence.

'I'd never have spotted that.'

'Stuart thought you might want to paint them yourself.'

'Good of Stuart.'

I'm not one for this kind of conversation, as you may imagine. The older I get, the more I just want people to be straightforward.

'So what do you think, Oliver?'

'What do *I think*?' He did the legs-apart, chin-in-fist, head-scratching National Gallery number again. 'I think it's a fine thing the two of you have cooked up together, that's what I think.'

I left him to it. I went to bed. Oliver slept in the spare room. It happens at times like this. If the girls notice, we say Daddy was working late and didn't want to disturb Mummy when he came to bed.

Stuart   I ran into Oliver in the yard. He immediately put down a tray of endive and went into an act of elaborate bowing and scraping. He wound the corner of a handkerchief round one finger which made the rest of it practically flap in my face. I was clearly meant to be reminded of something.

'Oliver,' I asked, 'What are you being?'

'Your valet,' he replied.

'Why?'

'Aha!' he exclaimed, screwing up half his face and tapping the side of his nose with his finger. 'Always remember, no man is a hero to his valet.'

'That's probably true,' I replied. 'But seeing as no-one actually has a valet nowadays, it strikes me as a rather irrelevant piece of wisdom.'

Oliver   In days of yore, before my master rescued me, I sank low. I sold tea-towels and oven gloves out of plastic stacking crates. I was a door-to-door runner for a video rental enterprise which may not have been strictly kosher. I pushed flyers through letter boxes. Including my own. Which was not as onanistic as it sounds. I realised that if, with a villainous shoulder-swirl to conceal the deed, I shoved fifty or more gaudy leaflets onto my own mat, then the householder was unlikely to complain and the load was suddenly lightened. I once posted through chez moi's vent an arguably supernumerary sheaf of special Tuesday night dinner offers for the Star of Bengal, who are equally proud of their dine-in facilities and their home-delivery expertise ('Curry in a Hurry'), and then the next day took advantage of the said offer and blew my paltry wage on squiring my Meilleure Demie to the said Candlelit Special. As I recall, we qualified for the free vegetable side dish with every order over £10.

Stuart would no doubt assert that I was being taught an elementary lesson on the nursery slopes of venture capitalism. Odd that I felt more like an unprotected wage slave being exploited by a major nickelfucker.

Plus ça change, eh?

Gillian   You might think this a betrayal. Oliver probably would. But I had a sudden flashback to when he had his depression. So I phoned Stuart at his office and said I was worried that Oliver was overworking. There was a silence, then a surprisingly harsh laugh, then another silence. Finally, Stuart said, 'In my opinion, Oliver thinks any sort of working is overworking.' He sounded as if he really despised Oliver and despised me too for being the little wifey ringing up the boss about her husband. He sounded like the boss as well: not an old friend – and ex-husband – but an employer and a landlord. Then he caught himself and started asking about the girls, and it was all back to normal.

I'm probably quite the wrong person to have to deal with a depressive. But that's not my fault, is it?

Oliver   By the way, it wasn't some Teutonic sage. The line about valets and heroes. It was Mme Cornuel. Heard of her? No, me neither. I looked her up. 'A *bourgeoise* famous for her mordant wit,' I read. 'Men of letters flocked to her *salon* in the late seventeenth century.' Ah, but why remember her any longer? Stuart has pronounced her wisdom 'irrelevant'. Let us erase her memory, let us delete her sole contribution to the dictionary of quotations, 'seeing as no-one actually has a valet nowadays'.

Ellie   It's not that I want it to 'get anywhere'. That's how parents talk.

It's just that it's perfectly clear it's 'going nowhere'. That's how parents talk as well. Of course.

Enjoy the moment. I do. Try different things. I do. Don't tie yourself down. I don't. You're only young once. I know. Enjoy your freedom. I try.

So it's no big deal. What did I tell Oliver when he tried to set me up? I said middle-aged divorcees weren't my scene. Or double-divorcees, as it turned out. And they aren't.

Look, I'm not in love with Stuart. Or likely to be. I go round to his place once a week, once every ten days. It's still as bare and undecorated as the first time. We usually go for a meal, have a nice bottle of wine. Afterwards we go back to the flat and sometimes I'll stay the night with him, sometimes we'll have a quick shag and I'll be off, sometimes we don't bother. You see? No big problem. It's not a high-maintenance relationship.

It's just that, if I *was* interested, really interested, I know I'd be getting hurt. And it makes me really pissed off to think about it. I ought to be pleased, oughtn't I? But I'm not. I'm really pissed off with him.

Do you know what's up? I mean, it seems obvious to me. As obvious as ... well, the fact that his flat is completely bare except for piles of shirts and piles of washing-up he leaves for the cleaner, and one of the reasons it's so bare is because he's always round at St Dunstan's Road putting up shelves and stuff.

Grown-ups are fuck-ups, right?

Sophie   Mum's been really weird lately. Staring out of the window like I said. Forgetting I've got music on Tuesdays. I think she's worried about Dad. Frightened about him getting Down in the Dumps again.

I tried to think of something to cheer her up. So I said, 'Mum, if anything happened to Dad, you could always marry Stuart.' Well, it seemed like a sensible idea, as he's got loads of money and we can never afford anything.

Mum just looked at me and ran out of the room. After a bit she came back and I could see she'd been crying. She also had that face which means we're going to have a Serious Talk About Something.

Then she told me what she'd never told me before. That Stuart and her were married before she married Dad.

I thought about this for a bit. 'Why didn't you tell me?'

'Well, we thought we'd tell you if you asked.'

That's not a real answer, is it? Like, oh, Mum, was Dad ever married to Princess Di, for instance, now that I know I have to ask before I'm told.

I thought about it some more, and it seemed obvious really. 'So you're trying to tell me that Stuart's my real father?'

Guess what? Lots more tears. Hugs. She told me it absolutely isn't true. You know that way Mum has of saying, 'It absolutely isn't true'?

Why didn't she tell us Stuart and her were married – unless there was a secret for some reason. What else can it be?

She said I wasn't to tell Marie. Perhaps they're waiting till she asks.

'Well,' I said, trying to be sensible, 'I suppose you could always marry him again.'

Mum said I wasn't to tell anyone else about it either.

But I *did* ask. Don't you remember? That night Dad came home drunk. I asked who Stuart was and Mum said he was just someone they knew. They could have told me then, couldn't they?

Stuart   Aren't there a lot of terrible stories in the newspapers nowadays? Did you see that case the other week about a man who'd been abused in a children's home, years and years ago? It's terrible when trust is betrayed, isn't it? And then time passes, and it doesn't get any better. This chap grew up, tried to forget it, couldn't, and twenty years later tracked down the . . . carer who'd done it to him. The fellow was in his sixties by now, so in a way their roles were reversed: he was at the mercy of someone stronger, just like the boy had been all those years before.

So he introduced himself to his abuser, took him for a drive and pushed him off a cliff. No, that makes it sound too clean. He let him pray first. That's interesting, isn't it? He let him kneel down and pray. He told the police afterwards that he would have spared him if he'd prayed for his victims, but all he did was pray for himself. So he dragged the old man to the cliff-top and booted him off. That's what he said, booted him off. He told the police he could show them the skidmarks where his victim had been trying to hang onto the ground. They couldn't find hide nor hair of the body. No, that's wrong, hair is what they did find, halfway down the cliff. A football scarf with some grey hairs on it. It was a Portsmouth scarf, I'll always remember that. Blue and white. Portsmouth.

It's a terrible story, isn't it? And it's more terrible when you think that to the murderer it probably felt like fair dos.

If anything, less than the old man deserved. If anything, he probably thought he'd let him off lightly.

The other thing I remember is that he told the police he was surprised by how calm he felt afterwards. He said he'd gone home, made himself a cup of tea and had a good night's sleep.

Oliver   Another thing. Mr Cherrybum's spirit level. I looked at it and thought: that's what we all need. Something with which to measure the level of our spirits. Lay it on the human soul,/ Watch the bubble in its bowl/ By its rise and fall betray/ Whether you are grave or gay.

16: Would You Rather?

Oliver   You know that game called Would You Rather? As in, would you rather be buried up to your neck in wet mud for a week or compare all the recorded versions of the New World symphony? Would you rather stroll down Oxford Street bollock-naked with a pineapple on your head or marry a member of the Royal Family?

Here's another one for you, one from real life. Would you rather your depression was endogenous or reactive? Would you rather that your gross and paralysing sensitivity to the pain and grief of existence were the fault of your genetic inheritence, of all those glum and grouchy ancestors you see lined up in the *rétroviseur*, or would you rather it were provoked by the world itself, by what are risibly referred to by The Men Who Guess as 'life events', as if an equal and opposite category of 'death events' also existed.

Endogenous: in the happy-clappy, kids'-colouring-book, politicians' view of life, we stand proudly on the shoulders of preceding generations, seeing further, breathing cleaner air. To those stricken by the sadness of things, however, the pyramid is inverted and those same ancestors weigh upon our shoulders, driving us into the ground like frail tent-pegs. Ah, the incluctable whipcrack of DNA: what is one but the final thread of a cat-o'-nine-tails wielded by some muscular pirate generations previously? And yet, therein lies hope: if our burden is biochemical, might it not therefore be magicked away by the boffins? We are about to enter the lair of Stuart's *bête noire*, genetic modification, which does not seem to me as *noire* as it's painted. A little tweak of a gene, a deft replaiting of that vital vegetable spaghetti which distinguishes Oliverness from Stuartness, and there you are: cheerier than Pops, less grumpy than Gramps. The black dog turns into a pussycat.

Reactive: or would you rather those blue-black days, that indigo inner landscape, were a direct and more or less reasonable response to the things that have happened in your own lifetime? Things that might deflate even Mr Cherrybum: for instance, the loss of your mother before the age of eleven, the death of your father, redundancy, illness, marital fracture, *und so weiter*? Because then you could argue to yourself that if only the world were to sort itself out, you could do likewise. However, if you are thinking clearly – which is unlikely, since your metabolic thought-rate will either have slowed to the plop of a grizzly's heartbeat during hibernation or else be whizzing along like the overture to *Russlan and Ludmilla* – you will perceive a logical problem here. If, say, one of the 'life events' which has nailed you to your bed is the death of your mother at the age of six, then it's hard to imagine how such a calamity gets unfixed, isn't it? A stepmother is no serotonin, as the saying has it. Equally, if you have been pole-axed by a redundancy notice, that is hardly the best position from which to apply for a job, is it?

Endogenous vs Reactive: still making up your mind? Bong, bong, bong. Time's up! And now I shift the goalposts. This binary-choice quizette was, I confess, a little bogus. Because The Men Who Guess have in recent times disowned their own famous distinction. Nowadays they propose that you may be gifted with a genetic propensity to be downcast by those naughty 'life events'. So: endogenous or reactive – you can have both! It could be you! It's all your mother's fault (and hers before her) – and then she dies as well! Suck on that, Mr Well-Balanced-on-a-Balcony. There is no either/or, there is only both/and. Which even the most wall-eyed observer of what the philosophers call life could have told you in the first place. Life, after all, does indeed consist of walking bollock-naked along Oxford Street with a pineapple on your head *and then* being obliged to marry a member of the Royal Family; of being buried up to the neck in wet mud while listening to all available recordings of the New World symphony.

The clever thing about depression, you see, is that it makes compatible what is outwardly incompatible. As in, none of it is my fault, and it's all entirely my fault. As in,

Islamic fundamentalists are releasing nerve gas into the London Underground to kill the city's entire population – but they're only doing it to get *me*. As in, if I can make jokes about it, I can't be depressed. Wrong, wrong! It's cleverer than you, and it's even cleverer than me.

Stuart   Sophie told me she thinks it's wrong to eat animals.

I explained about organic principles, the Soil Association, non-intensive husbandry, organic feed, animal welfare, and so on. I told her about all the things that are banned, from growth hormones to permanent tethering, from GM feed-stuffs to slatted concrete floors. I probably went on a bit.

Sophie said it was still wrong.

'Well, what are your shoes made of?'

She looked at them for a while, then back at me, and said, in a very grown-up way, 'I'm not proposing to eat my shoes, am I?'

Where did she get that from? 'I'm not proposing to ...' She sounded like a Prime Minister all of a sudden.

She stood there, waiting for an answer. I couldn't find one. I could only think of that film where Charlie Chaplin eats his shoes. But that's not an answer either.

Oliver   Gillian marks up the newspaper every morning. She has a red pen and puts ✳s by stories she thinks I might find interesting or amusing. What a trouper, eh?

Bound to work like breakfast cereal, isn't it? With added moral fibre, indeed.

But news delights me not, nor features neither. I do not even understand the concept of 'news' any more, I realise. It's an absurd plural to begin with. What's the singular – 'a' new? So the word ought to be 'the new', not 'the news'. The new as opposed to the old. Ah, the spirit of pedantry still flickers briefly in Oliver, you see.

My second beef. The new as opposed to the old. But it never is opposed, is it? The news always contains the oldest stories known to the tribe. Brutality, greed, hatred, selfishness, the four horsemen of the human soul ride across the broad screen applauded by the envious: this is the world news tonight, this morning, tomorrow, for all time. Cloying the gazettes with cant, well said, my friend.

So I have taken to reading those pages in which I have no interest. Item, the goings on among the horse-racing fraternity. Tales of fetlock and pastern. Who's putting up several pounds overweight (me! me!). Who thrives in muddy going (*pas moi! pas moi!*).

Here is a piece of sempiternal wisdom from the land of blinkers and binox: it is a known truth that the owner of an unraced two-year-old is never a candidate for suicide.

Isn't that so very fine?

The only question remaining is: who will buy me an unraced two-year-old?

Dr Robb   You listen. You are a witness. You validate. Sometimes just getting them to talk helps. But it takes courage to do so, to talk about the sort of feelings they're going through. Often more courage than they've got. Depression is full of vicious circles like this. As a doctor, you find yourself recommending exercise to someone who feels exhausted all the time. Or explaining research into the benefits of sunlight to someone who only feels safe lying in bed with the curtains drawn.

At least Oliver isn't a drinker. Cheering yourself up in the short term in order to depress yourself in the longer term. That's another vicious circle. And here's another. Sometimes – not often, and not in Oliver's case – you look at a person's life and think that, objectively, they're quite right to be depressed. You would be too if you were in their shoes. And then your job is to try and convince them they're wrong or mistaken to be depressed.

There was a report out recently which stated that people who are more in control of their professional lives are healthier than those who aren't. In fact, not being in control of your life was shown to be a more significant negative health indicator than drinking or smoking or other conventional factors. The newspapers made much of this, but it seems to me that such findings could be reached by anyone with a modicum of common sense. People who are in control of their working lives are likely to be closer to the top of the pile anyway. Probably better educated, more health-conscious, and so on. People who aren't in control of their lives are likely to be nearer the bottom of the pile. Less well educated, less well paid, more likely to have the sort of job that exposes them to health risks, and so on.

What's obvious to me, as a GP of twenty years' standing,

is that the free market operates in health just as it does in business. And I'm not talking about running hospitals on a commercial basis. I'm talking about pure health. Free markets make the rich richer and the poor poorer and tend towards monopoly. Everyone knows that. It's the same with health. The healthy get healthier, the unhealthy get unhealthier. More vicious circles.

I'm sorry, my partner would say I'm on my soapbox again. But if you saw what I see on a daily basis. I sometimes think at least plagues were more democratic in their effect. Except of course they weren't – because the rich were always better able to isolate themselves, or better able to run away. The poor were always wiped out.

Oliver   You recall that I was *un peu* hyper about the wallpaper? Afear'd o' reading the runes, of being panicked by a recurring pattern of madeleines, if you follow my *piste*. Funny thing was, when we moved in, there wasn't any. It'd all been painted over by the previous occupants. Who could imagine that the heart's salve could be as easily applied – indeed, turn out to be exactly the same thing – as a gallon or two of brilliant white vinyl matt emulsion?

But not so fast. The other day I was having a bad day, as we like to say – since to call the day bad is to blame the day for its malignity rather than stigmatise the endurer of the said day – one of those days when, nailed to the couchette, the prisoner of his own consciousness can find naught to fall back upon except the wide-screen entertainment of the wall.

At first I took it to be an ocular disturbance possibly occasioned by a gourmandising attitude to the dothiepin. A flawed diagnosis, rectified by the calling-in of a specialist – Matron herself – who confirmed that the hallucinatory Op Art before my eyes was none other – O trite yet brutal phenomenon – than the old wallpaper beginning to show through again.

You see how realism dogs us? How fruitless our efforts to muzzle the beast? Who was it said, 'Things and actions are what they are, and the consequences of them will be what they will be; why then should we desire to be deceived?' Bastard. Old eighteenth-century bastard. Deceive me, O deceive me – as long as I know it and like it.

Stuart   I think Oliver is completely losing it.

I said to him, 'Oliver, I'm sorry you're depressed.'

'It's moving house,' he replied. 'It's up there with death of the paterfamilias.'

'Is there anything I can do for you?'

He was sitting in his dressing-gown on the sofa in the kitchen. He looks terrible at the moment, all white and lethargic. Plump as well. Pills plus lack of exercise, I assume. Not that Oliver ever took anything but mental exercise. He isn't even taking that nowadays. His expression seemed to say that he wanted to be bitter and sarcastic but didn't have the energy.

'Actually, there is,' he said, 'old chum. You can buy me an unraced two-year-old.'

'A what?'

'It's some kind of nag,' he explained. 'It's more effective than Dr Robb's entire pharmacopoeia.'

'Are you serious?'

'Perfectly.'

He has lost it, hasn't he?

Gillian   Sophie has announced that she's a vegetarian. She says lots of her new friends at school are vegetarians. My immediate thought was I didn't want to have another picky eater in the house. Thinking about what Oliver will and won't eat at the moment is enough for me. So I asked Sophie – treating her in a very grown-up way, which she always responds to – I asked her if she would mind putting off the implementation of her decision – which of course I respected – for a year or two, because we seemed to have enough on our plate at the moment as it is.

'Enough on our plate,' she repeated, and laughed. I hadn't said it deliberately. Then – since I was treating her as a grown-up – she did me the honour of treating me as one in return. She explained that it was wrong to kill and eat animals, and once you had understood this, there was no choice except to be a vegetarian. She went on at some length about this – well, she is Oliver's daughter, after all.

'What are your shoes made of?' I asked, when she had finished.

'*Mum*,' she replied, with all a child's weary stubbornness, 'I'm not proposing to eat my shoes.'

Oliver   Jogging is recommended. Do you know Dr Robb, by the way? (Probably not, unless you are in the same *bateau ivre* as *moi*.) The Good Doctor only used the word exercise, but I heard jogging. I must have let slip a swaddled preference for the Oblomovian divan, so she explained. Exercise, according to this week's wisdom from The Men Who Guess, raises the sacred endorphin levels and so provokes a lifting of the spirits. Before you know where you are it's happy-bunny time again. QED.

My response was not Archimedean, I fear. I did not let slip the bathwater in exultation. I may even have whinnied my despair like a stressful slimline porker. Later, I reasoned it thus: the very adoption of jogging apparel, from cheesy trainers to cheesy smile via saggy-bummed two-piece with lurid zip, would so depress my endorphin levels to begin with, while the idea of showing myself thus arrayed in *daylight*, that other supposed mood-enhancer, would so fill me with shame, that I would have to pogo my way to Casablanca and back merely to restore this mythical substance to its original basement reading. QEFD, and you can work out the F for yourself.

Ellie   It's true what I said about Stuart. It's not a problem, it's not a big deal, it isn't high-maintenance. So why isn't it more straightforward?

We were back from a Chinese, and I was in one of those do-I-don't-I moods, when you want the other person to help make your mind up. But he wasn't playing. Either he wasn't picking up my mood or he was and it didn't bother him one way or the other. And I wanted to say: look, when we first met you were all grown-up, i.e. bossy, about things like me wanting cash and going out for a drink. Now you can't even tell me whether you want me to stay the night or not.

I said, 'So what do you think?' We were halfway between the front door and the bedroom.

'What do *you* think?' he answered.

I waited. I just waited. Then I said, '*I* think that if you don't know what *you* think, then *I* think I'm going to fuck off home.'

Now there are a few things you can say to that, but 'Fine' is fairly low on my list. And there are a few bits of body language you can go in for at the same time, but turning away to the bathroom to have a pee before I'm out of the front door is also low on my list.

The next morning I'm in the studio, both of us working away, and I suddenly lose it. There's Gillian, sitting at her easel, bending forwards, adjusting the lamp, in profile, like some calm bloody cut-out Vermeer, and I'm thinking: hey, *excuse me*, but didn't you and your second husband, the big fraud himself, didn't you try to get me off with your first husband without telling me you'd been married to him, and didn't he run this Mr Henderson scam on me, and then when I did end up shagging him didn't it soon become mega-obvious that while he was perfectly polite about shagging me and even seemed to enjoy it, he was still completely fucking obsessed with you over there?

So I told her. I told her in those words too. Have you noticed how grown-ups hate the word shag? My dad doesn't mind if I smoke and get cancer, that's fine by him, but when I once said I was shagging a boy, he looked at me as if I was a real slapper. Also, like I was failing to appreciate the beautiful act of making love like it had always been with my mum, blah blah, back in the days before they split up. So I deliberately said shag to Gillian, except she didn't even wince as I hoped, just carried on listening very carefully, and when I got to the bit about Stuart being completely fucking obsessed with her, you know how she reacted?

She smiled.

Stuart   I read about this case in the paper today. It's a truly horrible story, and I advise you to skip the next bit unless you've got a strong stomach.

It happened in the States, though it could have happened anywhere. I mean, America is just an exaggerated version of everywhere else, isn't it? Anyway, there was a man, fairly young, in his twenties, whose father died. His girlfriend was away on a cruise at the time, and she no doubt quite reasonably decided that since the father was dead rather than just dying, she would carry on with the cruise rather than cut it short in order to comfort her boyfriend. Now he – perhaps equally reasonably – resented this bitterly, with a bitterness that time didn't heal. It seemed like a terrible betrayal. So he decided to inflict as much pain on her as he had suffered himself. He wanted her to know the sort of grief he had felt at the death of his father.

Are you sure you want to go on? I'd bail out now if I were you. So he married his girlfriend, and they talked about starting a family, and she became pregnant and had the baby, and he waited long enough for her to be properly bonded with the child, and then he killed it. He put plastic wrap – what we call clingfilm – over the baby's face and left it to die. Then he came back, took the clingfilm off and turned the baby face down in its cot.

I warned you it was horrible. And then there's this. For several months, apparently, the mother thought it was a case of cot death. That's what the doctor had said. But one day her husband went to the police station and confessed to murder. Now, why do you think he did that? Guilty conscience? Maybe. I'm not sure I altogether believe in guilty consciences. Not much, not in cases I've seen. OK, perhaps there was a bit of that. But wasn't it about inflicting even more and even worse pain on his girlfriend-wife? If she thought it was a case of cot death, she could blame Fate or something. But now she knew it wasn't Fate. It was deliberate. Pain had been caused deliberately, by someone she thought loved her, to someone else she loved, with the sole purpose of hurting her. You could say that she found out what the world was like at that moment.

It was a terrible thing to do, wasn't it? I'm not saying it wasn't. But in a way, what was most terrible about it was that it was also, in a way, quite reasonable. In a terrible way, of course.

Oliver   The whipcrack of DNA. Rather pleased with that, I admit. Made me think. Man (not forgetting woman, neither). The being without a reasonable reason for being.

Gave himself a reason in the old days, in the time of myths and heroes. When the world was big enough for tragedy. Nowadays? Nowadays we just tippy-tip our toes in the circus sawdust to the whipcrack of DNA. What is human tragedy for today's diminished species? To act as if we have free will while knowing that we don't.

17: A Todger Among the Drachmae

Anonymous

TO WHO IT MAY CONCERN, TAX OFFICE N16 DISTRICT

This is to inform you that Oliver Russell of 38 St Dunstan's Road N16 is avoiding paying tax. He is employed by the Green Grocer company (head office Ryall Road N17) as a van driver and is paid in cash by the boss Mr Stuart Hughes. Russell and Mr Hughes are in point of fact old friends. We estimate that he is currently in receipt of £150 p.w. cash from Mr Hughes. We have reason to believe that Russell is also involved in the distribution of bootleg video rentals and leaflets advertising curry houses and other items. You will understand that in the circumstances I am unable to sign this letter except as –

A Concerned Member of The Public

Oliver Dr Robb's very nice, isn't she? As far as being very nice makes the slightest difference to anything.

She listens, except that I don't want to talk much.

She tells me that feeling you're never going to get better is part of the depression. I say feeling you're not going to get better sounds like the normal and natural consequence of not getting better.

She asks about loss of libido and I try to be gallant.

I do seek to please her, though. I answer yes to all her questions. Poor sleep yes, early waking yes, loss of interest yes, loss of concentration yes, loss of libido see above, poor appetite yes, tearfulness yes.

She asks me how much I drink. Not enough to cheer me up, I say. We talk units. It seems that alcohol is a depressant. But she worked out that I don't drink enough for it to be one in my case. Isn't that depressing?

She says that daylight helps counteract depression. I say: and life is the opposite of death.

I am making her sound like some tabulating bureaucrat, I realise. It is not my intention. She is a fine and toastworthy representative of The Men Who Guess. Indeed, were it not for my loss of libido . . .

She asks me about the death of my mother. Well, what can I say? I was six at the time. She died, and then my father started taking it out on me because she'd died. Beating me up and so on. Because I reminded him of her.

Yes, I can offer the usual vignettes from the distant bourn of childhood – The Scent As She Kissed Me Goodnight, and The Way She Ruffled My Hair, and Bathnight In The Old Home – but how many are truly mine and how many purloined from the Cyclopaedia of False Memory I cannot at this juncture discern.

Dr Robb asks me how she died. In hospital, I say. Not that I saw her. One week she was taking me to school each morning and picking me up each afternoon, and the next she was being lowered into the ground. No, I didn't see her in hospital. No, I didn't see her laid out Looking Even More Beautiful In Death Than She Had Done In Life.

I always assumed she had died of a heart attack, of something grown-up and mysterious. The what and the why perplexed me more than the how. And when in later years I asked for details, my halibut father would merely karaoke away to the big tune of grief and abandonment. 'She's dead, Oliver,' was all the Old Bastard would ever say, 'and the best of me died with her.' In this he was almost certainly telling the truth.

Dr Robb asked me, in the most condolent and circumlocutious way, if it was a credible hypothesis that my distant mother might have topped herself.

Things *are* getting serious around here, don't you think?

Sophie   The next time I got Stuart to myself, I put my plan into action.

I asked if I could talk to him, which I don't normally ask, so that got him listening.

I said, 'If anything happens to Daddy –'

He interrupted. 'Nothing's going to happen.'

I said, 'I know I'm not a grown-up. But if anything happens to Daddy –'

'Yes?'

'Then will you be my Daddy?'

I watched him carefully as he thought about this. He didn't look at me, so he didn't see how closely I was watching. In the end, he turned to me and gave me a hug and said, 'Of course I'll be your Daddy, Sophie.'

It's all perfectly clear to me now. Stuart doesn't know he's my father because Mummy never told him. Mum won't admit it, to me or to him. Dad's always treated me like his daughter, but he must suspect something, mustn't he? That's why he gets Down in the Dumps.

So it's all my fault.

Stuart   'What the *fuck* is this?'

Oliver was more animated than I'd seen him for quite a while. He was waving a letter in my face in a way that obviously made it impossible to see what it was. After a while he calmed down, or more likely got tired. I looked at the document.

'It's from the Inland Revenue,' I said. 'Enquiring whether you have any further sources of income apart from your employment at The Green Grocer, and whether you were in employment in the foregoing period while in receipt of benefit.'

'I can fucking read,' he said. 'You might remember that I was retranslating Petrarch while you were still running a bitten forefinger beneath the lurid banalities of your daily horoscope.'

Enough of that, I thought. 'Oliver, you haven't been evading tax, have you? The game really isn't worth the candle, you know.'

'You fucking Judas.' He stared at me, all unshaven and red-eyed and frankly not very healthy-looking. 'You fucking denounced me.'

This was a bit rich. 'Judas denounced Jesus,' I pointed out.

'So?'

'So?' I thought a bit, or at least pretended to think. 'You're probably right. Someone has denounced you. Now, let's be practical. What do you think they could have on you?'

He assured me that he hadn't been moonlighting while working for The Green Grocer because the said establishment was such a nickelfucking sweatshop that its employees were wrung dishcloths at the end of the working day. But it was true that previously, while claiming benefit, he had taken undeclared cash jobs: pushing flyers through people's doors, renting videos door-to-door for some mysterious Mr Big.

'Anyway, I've told you all this before.'

'Have you? I'm not sure you have.'

'I could have sworn I had.' Then he sat down and his shoulders sagged. 'Oh God, I can't even remember who I've told what to any more.'

Well, this never used to bother him in the old days. He was always quite happy to tell the same old story again and again. 'Let's try and think about this calmly,' I said. 'The Revenue have certainly got something on you. But to give them their due' – Oliver groaned as I said this – 'they are really only interested in collecting the unpaid tax. They aren't interested in the criminal side of things.'

'Oh, great.'

'But I think you ought to be more worried about the benefits side. They can be really nasty if they want. I wonder if the person who denounced you knows about the Benefits hotline? That could be awkward.'

Oliver groaned again.

'And I suppose we ought to be concerned about the VAT-man as well. This bootleg video thing, that's Customs and Excise. And they can be vicious. Powers of search and entry. Nothing they like more than breaking down your front door at five in the morning and taking up the floorboards. Let's hope this joker doesn't know about the VAT hotline.'

'The fucking Judas,' he repeated.

'Yes, well. It probably is someone in the office. Or maybe it's one of the other drivers. Just try and think, Oliver. Can you think of anyone who hates you?' I asked cheerfully.

Mme Wyatt   Sophie and Marie came over. Stuart arrived with them in his car. I make no comment, of course.

I have the lemon cake as always, which they like. But Sophie does not want any. She says she is not hungry. I ask her to eat to please me. She says she is too fat.

I say, 'Where, Sophie? Where are you too fat?'

She says, 'Here.' She indicates her waist. I look at her waist. I do not see her fat. I only see her deficiency of logic.

'That is only because you have made your belt more tight than usual,' I say.

Really.

Oliver   I was soft-shoeing it around the house and made a rare foray into our bedroom. It's on the top floor, offering a crane-shot of the street. Have I told you that? I expect someone has. Someone tells you everything, don't they? You can't keep a secret around here for a nano-second. A Judas under every cushion.

Sorry, I . . . anyway. There was this loud, pitiless whine from the mid-distance. With any luck, a genetically modi-fied heat-seeking monster hornet coming to give me the *coup de grâce.* But it was something worse. The *coiffeur* was having his way with Mrs Dyer's monkey-puzzle tree – no, as I watched, not the *coiffeur* but the *boucher.* Its witty fingers, noble arms, then limbless trunk were cruelly belaboured by the buzz-saw. I felt my spirits, such as they were, drain like bathwater. 'May her monkey-puzzle flourish like the green bay' – it seems but a minute since I pronounced my plea.

Is it an omen? Who can tell? In *le bon vieux tems,* when we skied laughingly upon the snows of yesteryear, an omen lived up to its adjective and was ominous. The shooting star that stirred the velveteen sky, the snowy owl that perched all night in the blasted oak, the corny wolves howling from the graveyard – we may not have known what the fuck they portended, but we could see they were portents. Nowadays the shooting star is only a neighbour's sky-rocket, the snowy owl is in a zoo, and the wolves are being retrained in howling before their release back into nature. Harbingers of doom? In our diminished kingdom, the broken mirror betokens only a resented trip to John Lewis for its replacement.

Ah well. Our signs and omens grow more local, and the distance between the portent and what it portends diminishes to nothing. You step in dogshit – that's the warning and the calamity all in one! The bus breaks down, the mobile phone doesn't work. A tree is chopped down. Perhaps it all only means what it means. Ah well.

Sophie   Pig. Fat pig.

Gillian   We haven't got the radio on this morning. And we're not speaking much since Ellie's outburst. (What did you make of that, by the way? Wasn't it peculiar? Where does all that resentment come from? I don't think any of us have treated her in anything other than an honest, grown-up way.) So there's this rather awkward silence, and when Ellie picks up her coffee mug there's a slight clink, because the mug has lost its handle and the noise is her ring against the china. Just a quiet, occasional noise, but it sets me off down the years. Ellie isn't married or engaged, and there doesn't seem to be anyone around except Stuart, and their relationship seems fairly casual (maybe *that*'s the source of her resentment), but she wears a ring on the third finger of her left hand. I used to do that at one time, as a way of saying keep off, of not explaining things, of conjuring up an imaginary boyfriend, of defending your space when you can't stand the sight of men for a few days. Or weeks. Or months.

Mostly it worked, and some little piece of junk you picked up from a market stall would have almost magical properties when it came to warding off unwelcome approaches. I've forgotten those times, of course. The times I remember are when it didn't work. When someone put himself foursquare in front of you and just went for you. Took no notice of the ring even if you waggled it in his face. Didn't suggest it was a ploy or anything – just refused to acknowledge it as a factor. Ignored the half-smile you put on your face to pretend you weren't taking him seriously. Ignored whatever signals you were giving out. Just stood there and gave it his best shot. You and me, starting here, starting now, what about it? That was the implication, anyway. And each time I found it incredibly exciting. Sexy, dangerous even. I'd be acting cool but I'd be boiling underneath. Which I expect they sensed.

Don't misunderstand me. I'm not one of those women who 'likes to be dominated'. The idea of a man storming into my life and taking control and sorting me out is not one of my fantasies. I'd rather sort myself out. And I don't like bullies, or defer to them. I'm talking about something different, about that moment when someone is suddenly there, and says, without using the words, 'It's me. It's you. That's all there is to say.' As if some vast truth is being guessed at before your eyes, and all you have to do is reply, 'Yes, I think it's true too.'

If it happened again I wouldn't be waggling a piece of junk from a market stall but a band of gold I've worn every day for over ten years. And of course there'd be warning bells, like there always were, except this time more like ambulance sirens. But don't we all want to hear, once again, those simple words: it's me, it's you. And someone waiting for the answer: yes, I think it's true too. And things swirling in your head, half-familiar things you can't at this point name, things to do with time and destiny and sex, and underneath, beginning to swell, some confident tune you hope will dance you away.

Here, now, there is silence, just the dab of a swab and the creak of a stool. And the gentle tap of Ellie's ring against her mug.

Stuart   I always expect to find Oliver with his face turned to the wall, but I suppose the thing about Oliver is that even if he's ill he knows what the cliché is and does the opposite. So he was lying in bed with his back to the wall. He's in this sort of boxroom at the top of the house, with a blanket pinned across the window because obviously they haven't had time to make curtains. There's a bedside light with a Donald Duck lampshade.

'Hello, Oliver,' I said, not really sure how to pronounce even those words. I mean, if someone's really ill, I know how to behave. Yes, I understand about depression being an illness, and all that. In theory, anyway. So I suppose I mean he's got an illness I don't know how to behave with. It makes me impatient, and a bit unsympathetic.

'Hello, old "chum",' he said in a vaguely sarcastic way which didn't bother me. 'Have you found me that unraced two-year-old yet?'

Was I meant to laugh? It's a question with no correct answer. 'Yes'? 'No'? 'I'm working on it'? So I didn't say anything. I hadn't brought any grapes, for that matter, or chocolates, or interesting magazines I'd finished with. I told him a bit about work. How we'd had the dent in his van beaten out. He didn't seem to mind one way or the other.

'I should have married Mrs Dyer,' he said.

'Who's Mrs Dyer?'

'O fickle of heart and faint of purpose . . .' Or something like that, in a sort of low gabble. I don't always pay full attention when Oliver isn't sticking to the point. I shouldn't think you do either.

'Who's Mrs Dyer?' I repeated.

'O fickle of heart and faint of purpose . . .' And so on for a bit. 'She lives at number 55. You once told her I had AIDS.'

A memory I hadn't bothered with for years came back. 'That old biddy? I thought . . .' I thought she'd be dead by now, I was going to say. Except you don't say 'dead' to people who are ill, do you? Except I don't think of Oliver as ill. No doubt I should but I don't. As I said.

The conversation rambled on like this, not exactly a meeting of minds. I thought both of us had probably had enough when Oliver turned on his back, like someone on their deathbed, and said, 'So have you worked it out yet, old "chum"?'

'Worked what out?'

Oliver giggled in a stupid sort of way. 'The secret of a good chip butty, of course. The point, my old *mucker*, is that the heat of the chips melts the butter on the bread so that it runs down your wrists.'

There wasn't much to say to that either, except that I consider a chip butty a pretty unhealthy form of sustenance. Then he grunted, as if that was enough putting on an act for one day. 'Gillian.'

'What about Gillian?'

'When you were in the hotel room,' he said, and though I've been in hundreds of hotel rooms since, I instantly knew the one he was referring to.

'Yes,' I said. My mind went back to a wardrobe door, swinging open again and again.

'And?'

'I'm not following you.'

Oliver gave a snort. 'Did you think, what you saw, from your hotel window, did you think, what you saw, it happened regularly, day in, day out?'

'I'm still not following you.' Or rather, I was, but I didn't want to.

'What you saw', he said, 'was done solely for your benefit. Gala performance. One matinée only. Work it out, old "chum".' And with that he did the thing I hadn't seen before and turned his face to the wall.

I worked it out. And let me say the taste was bitter. Extremely bitter.

What did I tell you? Trust leads to betrayal. Trust invites betrayal.

Oliver   Impossible to avoid, *de temps en temps*, those Thersites moments, don't you find? Days when you know the pustuled fool speaks true. War and lechery, war and lechery. Not to mention vanity and self-delusion. I have a new Would You Rather? by the way. Would you rather destroy yourself by lack of self-knowledge, or destroy yourself by its acquisition? You have, oh, a lifetime to ponder that one.

Ripeness is all, according to another canonical expert. We know the dream: the loamy soil, the cloud-dismaying sun, pole position on the branch, the slow concentration of flavour, that giveaway colouring of the skin, and then, oh such ripeness, that were an infant's dimpled pinkie to prise us upward for a nano-second, the umbilical stalk from which we perpend would part so unresentfully from the branch, and we would paraglide weightlessly down onto a fortuitous clump of hay, there to lie, ripe, replete, at ease with the holy cycle of living and dying.

But most of us are not like that. We are like the medlar, which passes from indigestible hardness to umber collapse in the space of an hour, so that the hunter-gatherers who first valued it, those early organicists, those proto-Stuarts, used to sit up through the night with tentative candle and urgent fruit net, waiting for the moment. But who watches the fruit-watcher? In our case, there is no attendant with nightlight aloft, and we snore through our blip of ripeness. Indurate middle-age the one minute, deliquescing senility the next.

Concentrate, Ollie dear, concentrate. You do so *wander*

nowadays. Look at that trail of ox-bow lakes behind you. What does the pustuled fool proclaim?

Only this. The sad truth quickly learnt by the humblest gerbil, but taking our own dumb species the full three-score-and-ten to apprehend. That all relationships, even between two pure novice nuns – hey, especially between two pure novice nuns – are about power. Power now. And if not power now, then power later. And the sources of power are so old, so familiar, so cruelly deterministic, so simple, that they have but simple names. Money, beauty, talent, youth, age, love, sex, strength, money, more money, yet more money. The Greek shipping tycoon in the men's room demonstrates to his chuckling compadre what the world is all about: he picks up the attendant's tip-saucer and lays his *membrum virile* across it. Look no further, O ye seekers after wisdom. The Greek's name was Aristotle, after all. And I bet he didn't get denounced to the Benefits Hotline.

So how does all this relate to the frankly less than Shakespearean *histoire* or *imbroglio* with which you have found yourself involved? My apologies, by the way, if you think such are required. (Are they? Didn't you, in a sense, *invite yourself in*? Weren't you, in a sense, *asking for it*?) Merely that there was a time when Gillian's lustre made her the cynosure of all eyes, when Ollie's flair – I put it no higher – carried the field before him, and when Stuart, if you'll pardon the phrase, couldn't get any if he paid for it. And now? Now Stuart can pay for it. Now it is Stu-baby's todger among the drachmae. You find my *Weltanschauung* grown simplistic? But life does simplify itself, you'll find, its grim lineaments do expose themselves as the years progress and disappoint.

Mind you, I'm not saying Stuart could pull Maria Callas. Were he to have yodelled 'I Remember You' at her, I doubt she would have responded with '*Di quell'amor ch'è palpito.*'

Stuart   Do you know the phrase 'Information wants to be free'? Computer people use it. I'll give you an example. It's very hard to get rid of information you store in your computer. I mean, you can press that delete key, and think it's vanished for ever, but it hasn't. It's still there on the hard drive. It wants to survive and it wants to be free. The Pentagon says you have to overwrite information on the hard drive seven times before it's obliterated. But then there are data recovery companies who claim they can get back data which have been overwritten even as many as twenty times.

So how can you make sure of destroying the information? I read somewhere that the Australian government uses gangs of beefy men with large sledgehammers to smash up their hard drives. And the bits have to be so small that they can be fed through a sort of grille with a really narrow gauge. Only then can the authorities be certain that nothing can be recovered, that the information is finally dead.

Does that remind you of anything? It does me. They'd have to get beefy men with sledgehammers to smash up my heart if they wanted to make sure. That's what they'd have to do.

I know this is a comparison. But I happen to think it's true.

18: Comfort

Gillian   It happened like this. Oliver managed to rise from his bed shortly before it was time for supper. He didn't have any appetite – he doesn't at the moment – and said very little as we ate. Stuart cooked a *piperade*. Oliver made some joke about it, which could have been hurtful, but Stuart wisely didn't take much notice. We just sipped at a glass of wine – Oliver didn't even touch his. Then he got up, made a vague sign of the cross over the table, said something Oliverish, and added, 'Now I shall drag myself back to my wankpit so that you may talk amongst yourselves about me.'

Stuart stacked the dishwasher. As I watched him I drank half Oliver's wine. He was realigning the plates that were already in the machine, which he always does. He once told me about maximising water flow, and I told him never to use the phrase again in my hearing. But I was laughing as I said it. Now he stacks in a sort of exaggeratedly deliberate way, frowning and pausing. It's quite funny, if you can imagine it.

'Does he wank?' Stuart suddenly asked.

'Not even that,' I replied without thinking. And in any case, that was hardly much of a betrayal, was it?

Stuart filled the powder tray, closed the door and gave the dishwasher a pitying look. I can tell he wants to buy me a new one. I can also tell he's holding back from mentioning the subject.

'Well, I'll just pop in on the girls,' he said. He removed his shoes and set off upstairs. I carried on drinking Oliver's wine and looked at Stuart's shoes on the kitchen floor. A pair of black loafers, pointing out at an angle of ten to two, as if he'd just stepped out of them. Well, he had, of course, that was true – I mean, it was as if the shoes still had life in them somehow. They weren't new, they were worn in, with creases across the top, and vertical wrinkles down the sides. Everyone wears his or her shoes in a different way, don't they? Worn shoes must be like fingerprints, or DNA, to the police. And shoes are like faces, too, aren't they? The creases where they bend, the crow's feet that develop?

I didn't hear Stuart come downstairs again.

We drank the rest of the wine.

We weren't drunk, though. Neither of us. I'm not using that as an excuse. Do I want an excuse?

He kissed me first. But that's not an excuse either. A

woman knows how not to be close enough if she doesn't want to be kissed.

I did say, 'Ellie?'

He said, 'I've always loved you. Always.'

He asked me to touch him. It didn't seem much to ask. The house was quite quiet.

He began touching me. His hands on my legs, then under my knickers.

'Take them off,' he said. 'Let me touch you properly.'

He was on the sofa, his trousers halfway down his thighs, his cock standing. I was in front of him, holding my knickers. I somehow didn't want to put them down. His hand was through my legs, his wrist could feel I was wet and his fingers were on the base of my spine. He wasn't pulling me towards him: I was the one who moved. I felt twenty. I lowered myself onto his cock.

I thought – no, at those moments it's barely a thought, it's more something that passes through your mind, something for which you're hardly responsible – I thought: I'm fucking Stuart, and it doesn't matter because it's Stuart. At the same time, I also thought, I'm not fucking Stuart, because – if you want to know, if you must know – we'd never done it like that before, two hot kids in a kitchen, half-dressed, whispering, urgent.

'I've always loved you,' he said. He looked up into my eyes and I felt him come.

Before he left, he set off the dishwasher.

Stuart   I'm sorry for people who are sick. I'm sorry for people who are poor through no fault of their own. I'm sorry for people who hate their lives so much they kill themselves. I'm not sorry for people who are sorry for themselves, people who are self-indulgent, people who exaggerate their problems, people who waste your time and theirs, people who think that not doing anything except cry into their soup for weeks on end is more interesting than anything you or anyone else might have done in the intervening period.

I made a *frittata*. Gillie thought it was a *piperade*. The ingredients are the same, but with a *piperade* you stir the egg mixture as it cooks. With a *frittata*, you leave it to itself until it's cooked through, then put it under the grill. You don't need to brown the top, just cook it until it's solid, and then with a bit of luck, if you've done it right, you'll find that it's just a touch sloppy in the middle. Actually, not in the middle, but about a quarter to a third of the way in from the top. I got it right this time. I'd made it with asparagus tips, fresh peas, baby courgettes, parma ham and small cubes of fried potato. I saw that the first mouthful made Gill smile. But she didn't have time to say anything because Oliver announced wearily, 'My omelette's overcooked.'

'It's meant to be like that,' I said.

He pushed at it with his fork. 'Looks more to me as if the law of unintended effect has been applied.' Then, very deliberately, he began picking the vegetables out of the egg and eating them in an obnoxious way.

'Where do the peas come from at this time of year?' he asked in a tone of voice which implied that he couldn't care less. He looked at the pea on the end of his fork as if he'd never seen one before. Personally, I thought he was faking it. Most of it, anyway. Just because you're depressed, it doesn't mean you're suddenly going to start telling the truth, does it?

'Kenya,' I said.

'And the courgettes?'

'Zambia.'

'And the asparagus tips?'

'Peru, actually.'

Oliver slumped his shoulders with each answer, as if air-freight were some international conspiracy bent on perse-cuting him.

'And the eggs? Where do the eggs come from?'

'The eggs, Oliver, come out of a chicken's bum.'

That shut him up for a bit at least. Gill and I talked about the children. I quite wanted to tell her about my possible new pork supplier, but for Oliver's sake I thought I'd better avoid business. Sophie and Marie have settled into their new schools really well. I must say, it's been for the best. You might have read about the educational task force the Government sent into the borough where they used to live. Not the actual school the two of them were at, but even so. I wouldn't be surprised if they were next for the chop.

It was just a quiet domestic evening. I cleared the plates and brought in the rhubarb. I'd stewed it with some orange juice and zest, and made enough so that the girls could have some the next day, if they wanted. I'd just said something to this effect when Oliver got to his feet, leaving his bowl untouched, and announced he was going to bed. I gather this is par for the course nowadays. He doesn't do anything all day, goes to bed early, sleeps ten or twelve hours, and wakes up tired. It sounds like a vicious circle.

I finished clearing away and looked in on the girls. When I came downstairs again, Gill hadn't moved. Not an inch. She looked miserable, to tell the truth, and I suddenly had a horror of *her* falling into a depression as well. I don't know if this is a recognised pattern. I know it happens with alcoholics: one person turns into one, and then their partner, even if they don't want to, even if they hate the idea, turns into one as well. Maybe not straight away, but it's a real danger. They say alcoholism's an illness, so I suppose you can catch it, one way or another. And why not the same with depression? After all, it must be terribly depressing dealing with someone who's depressed, mustn't it?

So I put my arm round her and said – well, I can't remember. 'Cheer up, love,' or something like that. I mean, you can only say simple things in those circumstances, can't you? Oliver, of course, would find complicated things to say, but I really don't regard Oliver as an expert on anything nowadays.

Then we comforted one another.

Well, in the obvious way.

However else?

Oliver   Stuart bores me. Gillian bores me. I bore me.

The girls don't bore me. They are too innocent for that. They have not yet reached the age of choice.

Do you bore me? Not exactly. But you're not much sodding help either.

I bore *you*. Don't I? It's all right. You don't have to be polite. What harm can another pinprick do to a burst balloon? Perhaps I might be interesting as a test case, a counter-example. Watch Ollie fuck up his life, go thou and do not likewise.

I used to think there was a point to being me. Now I'm not convinced any more. I feel bloated and stupid. Sometimes I feel as if I've retreated to some control cabin deep within me, and am only connected to the outside world by periscope and microphone. No, that makes me sound as if I'm functioning as I'm meant to. As if I'm a machine. *Control* cabin – nothing could be further from the truth. You know that dream where you're driving along in a car, except the steering wheel doesn't work – or rather, it works just enough for you to still believe in it, which is a big mistake – and the same with the brakes and the gears, and all the time the road's descending and you're going faster, and sometimes the roof starts pressing down on you and the driver's door pushing in so that you can barely turn the wheel or reach the pedals . . . we've all had that dream, or some version of it, haven't we?

I don't talk much; I don't eat much, ergo I don't shit much. I don't work; I don't play. I sleep; and I feel tired. Sex? Remind me what the point of that is, I seem to have forgotten. I also seem to have lost my sense of smell. So I can't even nose myself. Sick people smell bad, don't they? Perhaps you can sniff me and tell me the news. Is that too much to ask? Ah, I can see it is. Sorry I spoke. Sorry I *imposed*.

This is all misleading. You probably think – if you can be bothered – after all, if I were you I wouldn't bother to think about me – but were you to, you might come to the conclusion that as long as I can describe my condition with relative lucidity, then 'things can't be that bad'. Wrong, wrong! 'His condition is hopeless, but not serious' – who said that? Add memory loss to my list of symptoms. I can't be relied upon to remember to do it myself.

No, that's the catch in all this. I can only describe what is describable. What I can't describe is indescribable. What is indescribable is unbearable. And made the more unbearable by being indescribable.

Don't I make pretty patterns with words?

Death of the soul, that's what we're talking about.

Death of the soul, death of the body: Would You Rather? At least that's an easy one.

Not that I believe in the soul. But I believe in the death of something I don't believe in. Am I making sense? If not, then at least I'm giving you a tiny glimpse into the incoherence which enfolds me. Enfold: that's much too orderly a verb for where I am. All verbs are too orderly nowadays. Verbs seem like instruments of social engineering. Even *to be* is fascistic.

Ellie   Grown-ups are fuck-ups, right? And another thing, I hate the way they pretend you're one of them for as long as it suits them, and then when it doesn't you don't exist any more. Like when I told Gillian about Stuart being crazy for her and she just gave that little smile to herself like I wasn't there. Class dismissed.

I can't stay in this house, working away like nothing ever happened. As I said, it's not a problem. It was never a big deal with Stuart. But that doesn't mean I want to watch him prancing around in his home decorator's kit for the next few years. And watch *her* looking like a cat who's about to get the cream. You wouldn't stick around, would you?

Still, at least I've learnt some stuff from Gillian. And at least I didn't fall in love with Stuart. That's a comfort.

Mrs Dyer   Do you see what he's done? He must have been one of them cowboys they've been warning us about. He promised to fix the gate, and the bell, and chop down the tree for me and cart it away. So he chopped it down and left it lying there so I can't get out the front door and went to get a van. He said he had to hire a van specially as the tree turned out bigger than he thought, so I paid him in cash and he went away and never came back. He didn't fix the gate or the bell. He was a very pleasant young man but he turned out to be a cowboy.

When I rang the Council they said what was I thinking of, having a tree cut down without their permission and they wouldn't be surprised if someone wanted to prosecute. I said you'd better come and prosecute me in the next world then. That's the only place I'll get any p and q.

Mme Wyatt   I still want everything I said I wanted. And I know that I shall get none of it. So I take comfort from that well-cut suit, that sole off the bone, that book written with a good style which does not have an unhappy ending. I shall value politeness and short conversations, and I shall want things for others. And I shall always feel the pain and the wound of the things that I had and that I still want and that will never come again.

Terri   Ken took me to Obrycki's for a crab feed. They give you a little hammer, a sharp knife, a pitcher of beer and a garbage bag at your feet. I knew what to do, but I let Ken show me anyway. Crabs are amazing constructions, like some modern piece of packaging invented way back when. You pick one off the pile, flip it over, look for a kind of top-pop on the underside, insert your thumbnail, rip it off, and the whole package just breaks in half. Then you snap off the claws, flip out the crummy meat, break the remaining core in half, insert a knife, loosen everything up a bit, cut across it, then dig in with your fingers and eat. We got through a dozen crabs with no sweat. Six each: there's a lot you throw away. I had a side order of onion rings and Ken had fries. Then to finish he ordered a crab-cake.

No, you don't know Ken.

And you don't need to worry about me from now on. Assuming you were.

Sophie   Stuart came up and kissed us goodnight.

Marie was fast asleep, and I pretended to be. I pressed my face into the pillow so he wouldn't smell any sick. When he'd gone, I lay there thinking of all the things I wished I hadn't eaten. Thinking how fat I am, what a disgusting pig I've become.

I waited to hear the front door shut. You can always hear it because it needs an extra pull. I don't know how long I stayed awake. An hour? More? Then finally I heard it.

They must have been discussing Daddy. He's seriously Down in the Dumps. Except I think we ought to call it by a grown-up name.

Stuart   When I said 'we comforted one another', that probably gave the wrong impression. As if we were a couple of old things, snuffling into one another's shoulders.

No, the truth is, we were like a couple of kids. It was as if something – from years and years before – had finally been released. It was also as if it was still back then, when we first met, as if we were starting again in a different way. When you're thirty you can be all sort of fake-grown-up. We were a bit like that, to tell the truth. We were serious, and had fallen in love, and were planning our lives together – don't laugh – and all of that fed into the sex, if you know what I mean. There wasn't anything wrong with the sex we had back then, but it was sort of *responsible*.

And I'd like to make another thing clear. Gillian knew exactly what we were up to, from the start. When I took off my shoes and said I'd just pop in on the girls, do you know what she answered?

'You can pop in on all three of them while you're about it.'

And there was a look in her eye as she said it.

When I got down she looked a bit moody and quiet, but I could feel she was all jumpy and expectant underneath, as if for once she didn't know what was going to happen in her life next. We drank some more of the wine, and I told her I liked the way she's doing her hair nowadays. She puts a scarf in it but it isn't the way American women put scarves in their hair. It isn't like a ribbon either. It looks artistic without being pretentious, and – being Gill – the colour of the scarf had been chosen to set off the colour of her hair perfectly.

She turned as I said it, and naturally I went to kiss her. She sort of half-laughed, because my nose had bumped into her cheek, and said something about the girls, but I was kissing the side of her neck by now. She turned as if to say something else, but in turning her lips came virtually onto mine.

We kissed some more, then stood up and half looked around as if wondering what to do next. Except that it was perfectly obvious what we were both after. It was also clear that she wanted me to take the lead, to be the boss. And that was nice, and exciting too, because when we'd been together before it had always been, I don't know how to put it, sex by consent. What do you want? No, what do you want? No, what do *you* want? A jolly decent to-and-fro, and fair, and all that, but a real turn-off nowadays, I find. What Gill was saying was, go on, let's have a different sort of sex. My guess is – I didn't think of it then, I was too involved in what we were doing – my guess is she thought that if I took the lead, this would make her feel less guilty towards Oliver. Not that this seemed to be a factor at the time.

So it was one of those scenes where I was touching her and pulling her and talking her into it all the time. And she was playing not exactly hard to get, but like, Convince me. So I convinced her over to the sofa, and as I say it was like kids' sex, getting at bits of one another, trying to undo your belt with one hand while being busy with the other, stuff like that. A bit of push-me, pull-me, and little things we hadn't done before. For instance, I quite like being bitten. Not heavy stuff, but a serious nip or two where the flesh is meaty. At one point I had the side of my hand in her mouth and was saying, 'Go on, bite me.' And she did, hard.

And then I was inside her and we were fucking.

But the thing about sofas is they're really designed for kids. Especially old broken-down sofas like this one. So we were kids on it for a bit. But anyone who's ever had a tweak in their back or got used to proper beds doesn't find the terrain so hospitable any more. So after a while I got both arms round Gillie and rolled us onto the floor. She hit it with a bit of a bump, but I wasn't going to be knocked out of her, not for anything. And that's where we stayed till we came. Both of us, by the way.

Gillian   It didn't happen as I said it did. I wanted you to keep the good opinion you have of Stuart – assuming you do. Perhaps I was working out the last bit of guilt I felt towards him. The way I told it to you is the way I would have liked it to happen, if I knew it was going to.

When he came downstairs, he said, 'The girls are fine.' Then he added, 'I looked in on Oliver too. He's wanked himself to sleep.' Stuart said this a bit brutally and it ought to have made me feel sorry for Oliver, but it didn't.

We were drunk, of course. Well, I was more than a bit. I usually stop at one glass nowadays, but I must have had nearly half a bottle by the time Stuart reached across and made a grab for me. I'm not using that as an excuse. Not for him either.

He got me half round the waist and his nose thumped into my cheekbone hard enough to make my eyes water, then I turned my lips away from his.

'*Stuart*,' I said, 'don't be silly.'

'*This isn't silly.*' He reached his other arm across me and seized my breast.

'The girls.' This might have been a tactical mistake, I admit, as if they were the main impediment.

'They're asleep.'

'Oliver.'

'Fuck Oliver. *Fuck Oliver*. But that's just it – you don't fuck Oliver, do you?' The way he said it didn't sound like Stuart – or not the Stuart I'd known.

'That's none of your business.'

'It is at this very moment.' He dropped his hand from my breast to my legs. 'Come on, fuck me. Fuck me for old times' sake.'

I began standing up, but I was a bit off-balance, and he used that, and I was suddenly on the floor with my head against one of the sofa legs, and Stuart was on top of me. I thought: this doesn't feel like a joke. His knee was pushing mine apart. 'I'll scream, and someone will come,' I said.

'They'll think you're fucking me,' he replied. 'They'll think you're fucking me because you don't fuck Oliver any more.'

He was pressing the air out of me with his weight, and I opened my mouth. I don't know if it was to scream or not, but Stuart shoved the side of his hand between my teeth.

'Go on, bite.'

Part of me couldn't take it seriously. I mean, this was Stuart, after all. The words Stuart and rape – or something approaching it – simply don't go together. Didn't. And at the same time I was thinking it was a sort of cliché. Not that I'd been in that position before. But part of me wanted to say, in a matter-of-fact voice: look, Stuart, just because Oliver and I aren't having much sex at the moment that doesn't mean I want to fuck you, or anyone else for that matter. If you're twenty and not having sex, you think about it most of the time. If you're forty and not having sex, you stop thinking so much about it and worry about other things instead. And you certainly don't want it like this.

He got my skirt up. He got my knickers off. Then he fucked me, with my head hard against the wood of the sofa. I smelt dust. He had his hand in my mouth all the time. There didn't seem any point in biting it.

I didn't panic. And I wasn't remotely excited by it. He hurt me a bit. He didn't break anything. He just fucked me against my will and against my choice. No I didn't bite, no I didn't scratch, no I haven't any bruises to show except one just above my knee, which proves nothing. Not that I need to prove anything. This isn't going to court. That's my choice.

No, I don't think I 'owed' it to Stuart for the way I treated him ten years ago.

No, I wasn't exactly frightened. It was Stuart, after all, I kept saying to myself, it wasn't a hooded stranger in a dark alley. I loathed it, and you could say I was bored by it at the same time. I thought: is this what they all want? Even the ones who seem nice? Is this what they'll all do, regardless of you?

Yes, I do consider it to have been rape.

I thought that, being Stuart, he would apologise. He just left me lying on the floor, got up, fixed his trousers, went across and set off the dishwasher, then left.

Why didn't I tell you this before? Because things have changed.

I'm definitely pregnant. And it can't be Oliver's.

19: Question Time

Stuart   I think you might be right. I'm certainly prepared to consider the matter. You see, when organic wines first started being produced, they weren't of very good quality. They just seemed a bit cranky. And then there was biodynamism – and *that* seemed even crankier, following the cycles of the moon and so on. I think one of the problems is that when people open a bottle of wine, they don't have the same health awareness as when they buy a bunch of carrots. But wine-making skills have improved across the board, and there's some decent organic stuff around. I'll definitely have another look at it. Anything that helps promote one-stop shopping is good in my book. As long as it's one-stop shopping at The Green Grocer.

Gillian   You're asking me to go back ten, twelve years.

You understand how I fell in love with Oliver, but you don't understand 'how or if' I fell out of love with Stuart? Well, just asking that question answers half of it. If you understand 'how' I fell in love with Oliver, then you understand 'how' I fell out of love with Stuart. One thing blots out the other. A loud noise drowns out a quieter one. No, let's not go in for comparisons. When someone claims to be in love with two people at the same time, in my opinion that means they're only half in love with each of them. If you're wholly in love with one, you don't notice the other. The question doesn't arise. If you've been in my position you'll understand. If not, you'll go in for mathematics.

'If' is the more interesting question. Stuart never behaved badly towards me. He tried to interfere with our wedding – but that was never going to be a straightforward day anyway. And even though I hurt him badly, he was practical and helpful – no, generous – all through the break-up. Insisted that I keep on the studio. Didn't contest the divorce as he could have done. And so on. I never saw him as an enemy, or an obstacle. When I did think about him, my feelings were always . . . positive. He was someone who had loved me and never mistreated me.

Until the other night. I still can't find a way of thinking about the other night. It was such a terrible betrayal of all I thought about Stuart.

Oliver   Byron. George Gordon, Lord. Didn't you even

231

recognise *that*? 'I want a hero . . .' Arguably – no *un*arguably one of the most famous opening lines in the history of . . . history.

Mme Wyatt   Why are you so curious about my marriage? It was all a long time ago. It is – how do you say it? – 'all done and dusted'. It is – that expression Stuart taught me – 'blood under the bridge'. I think I do not remember his name any more. As one of your fine aristocratic ladies put it, 'Intromission is not introduction.' I have my daughter. She was not exactly a virgin birth, true, but – no, I think I do not remember his name any more.

Ellie   Course I'm not telling you what Stuart's like in bed. You'd only ask him the same about me. And so on. Anyway, the sex had nothing to do with it. With the rest of it, I mean.

Gillian   Why should I be jealous of Ellie? That doesn't make any sense.

Stuart   No. We may not have parted on the best of terms. But . . . no. It's private.

Mme Wyatt   *Quelle insolence!*

232

Gillian   Yes, I have read Oliver's screenplays. They're very good, actually. In my opinion. Which is not one that counts. My only criticism would be that they're not simple enough. You know when songwriters try to be too clever – it's the music that should draw the attention, not the words. Don't you agree?

One was about Picasso, Franco and Pablo Casals taking part in a *pelota* competition just before the Spanish Civil War. Some people definitely liked it, but no-one could raise the money. 'Where's the babe interest?' That was one comment that rankled. So he wrote *Mountain Charlie*, based on a true story about a woman who dressed as a cowboy. But they said it lacked sparkle, so he rewrote it as a musical, a *Girl of the Golden West* for the new millennium. And then he did a prequel to *The Seventh Seal* . . . Well, it's the old story, isn't it?

Sophie   About an hour, maybe less. I told you. Then the dishwasher went off, then the front door banged, then I heard Mum come upstairs and creep past our door in case she woke me up.

No, I didn't hear anything 'odd'. Why should Mum be crying?

Stuart   Yes, of course it's true about Skullsplitter. I wouldn't have you on. It really does come from the Orkneys. You ought to try it one day.

Mme Wyatt   That is very well observed from your part. Yes, my name is Marie-Christine. Yes, my husband – the miserable one who I no longer remember – ran away with a girl, a tart, called Christine. And my second granddaughter is called Marie. But no-one can possibly know all these three facts except me. And you. So it is all a coincidence, in my opinion.

Stuart   Yes, I expect my parents would have been proud of me. But that's neither here nor there. They were always a bit disappointed in me when they were alive, and looking back I realise that didn't help my self-confidence when I was a kid. And they died when I was twenty. So it's all a bit late for them to start being proud of me.

   If ever I have children, I'm going to make sure I never undermine them the way I was undermined. I don't think they should be spoiled, but I do think they should be given a sense of their own worth. I'm sure that's easier said than done, but still.

   My *sister*? Funnily enough, I *have* tracked her down. She married an ear doctor and lives in Cheshire. I called in one afternoon when I was up that way. Nice house, three children. She's given up work, of course. We got on OK. Rather like we did as kids. Not badly, not well, just OK. And I certainly didn't tell *her* what's been going on in my life recently. So it's no good asking her.

Gillian   Sophie? No, Sophie's fine.

Mme Wyatt   Sophie? Well, adolescence has begun, no? Nowadays it begins at ten. She is a very conscientious girl, she wants very much to please. That has always been her nature. But who can resist adolescence?

Stuart   No, I never did hang the painting. In fact, I took it back to the shop I'd bought it from. They said they didn't want to buy it back from me. Not at any price. Meaning – we found the only mug who would take it off our hands when you walked in, and we don't think we'll ever find another one.

What's it of? I don't remember. A sort of view of the countryside, I think.

Ellie   It was so dirty I thought at first it was a Nativity. As I cleaned it, it turned into a farmyard scene. A cowshed, a cow, a donkey, a pig. The work of a talented amateur, as they say, i.e. not worth the canvas it's painted on.

Oliver   *That* old chestnut? That *vieux marron glacé*? No, really not, drearly not. Never a stir in that direction. Of course, no prejudice, some of my best friends and all that – actually, *none* of my best friends, come to think of it – unless – you're not hinting, are you? – Stuart? – it's a theory – you mean he crossed to the sunny side of the street when he was in the States – or before – makes sense in a way – two mayfly marriages – and he did look peculiarly ill at ease with Ellie when I tried to set them up. Well, well, well. Now that I glance in my moral *rétroviseur*, it all makes sense.

Terri   I'm outta here. But this time, it's my choice, not Stuart's. I don't owe you guys anything. Work things out for yourselves.

Dr Robb   I don't know. I can't predict. It's a depression of moderate strength. I'm not making light of it. But I don't think he's actively suicidal. He's not hospitalisable. Not yet. We'll keep the dosage at 75mg for the present and then reconsider our options. This isn't an illness you can predict, especially not with a patient like Oliver.

For instance, I was trying to get him to talk the other day. He was lying on his back in a fairly lethargic state, not really responding, and I mentioned his family background again – meaning his mother – when he turned towards me, suddenly all focused, and said in a flirting sort of way, 'Dr Robb, you're in a much higher risk category than me.'

It's true – some of the highest risk categories in developed Western countries are doctors, nurses, lawyers and those in the hotel and bar trade. And women doctors are higher-risk than male ones.

But I do think he's in a fragile state. I wouldn't like to predict what might happen if he took another blow.

Gillian   I've no idea whether or not Oliver's mother killed herself. The fact is, I only met his father once, and never having heard the theory in the first place, I was hardly likely to bring it up on such an occasion, was I? He seemed a nice enough old boy, though it was rather fraught, as you might expect. Oliver had prepared me to expect a monster, and when I didn't get one I naturally thought he was a lot nicer than he necessarily was. Also, I had a feeling that Oliver was, if not boasting about me, at least presenting me to his father in a competitive way. I suppose that's normal. Look what I've got – that sort of thing. His dad just sucked on his pipe and didn't rise to the bait, which I suppose was a relief.

When Dr Robb asked me if I knew anything, I said I'd look in Oliver's files for the death certificate. Actually, 'files' is an exaggeration. Oliver's got a small cardboard box labelled 'Ancestral Voices', which I dug out after he'd gone to bed one night. It's all he's kept of his family. A few photographs, a copy of Palgrave's *Golden Treasury* with his mother's name and a date in it – I think she won it as a recitation prize at school – a small brass hand-bell which he once explained to me, a leather bookmark of oriental design, an extremely battered Dinky toy – a cream and maroon double-decker bus, if you really want to know – a silver spoon which might have been a christening present except I never knew Oliver had been christened. Anyway, the point is – no death certificate. His father's is there, in an envelope marked 'Proof'.

I suppose we could send off to Somerset House for a duplicate, but how would that help? Lots of suicides are covered up, so it wouldn't necessarily answer the question.

In fact, it might mislead us. And if it did say death by suicide, well, that would be just too grim, wouldn't it?

Yes, you're right. If there had been a suspicion of suicide, there would have been an inquest, and according to Oliver one week she was alive and the next week she was being buried, so would there have been time? Except he was only six when it happened, and we know how approximate Oliver's sense of chronology is, don't we? So that doesn't get us much further.

Stuart   Me? Why would I risk having my own firm investigated by the Revenue?

Gillian   I don't know. I suppose it depends on Oliver's condition. We can't expect Stuart to go on paying his wages indefinitely. And I'd never accept charity from Stuart. Especially not now.

Oliver   *I*'ve a question for *you*. Anyone know how long it takes for a monkey-puzzle to grow full size? I need a tethering-pole for my unraced two-year-old.

Marie   Going to call him Pluto.

Oliver   Another question. Would you rather? Love or

be loved? You can only choose one or the other! Tick, tock, tick, tock, BONG! Decision time!

Stuart   No, you certainly can't see the photograph.

Ellie   I'll tell you one thing about Stuart, though. You remember where he lives? All those service flats and narrow streets and residents' parking bays. Know what he did when I first stayed the night with him? Over breakfast? Gave me a handful of parking vouchers so I wouldn't get clamped. I must have looked puzzled because he then started explaining how to use them. You take a coin, scrape off the day, hour, minute of your arrival, blah blah.

I knew that already. That wasn't why I was looking puzzled.

Gillian   No, I don't want to 'trace my father'. I'm not an orphan. He knew me, he left me.

Oliver   Another question for you. *Know* it's against the rules. Fuck the fucking rules. Gillian. The sainted one, the light of my life. Certainly been manipulating *me* all these years. Not to mention Mr Cherrybum. Shelves, even. The plutocrat with the spirit level. Point is – *question* is – how much has she been manipulating you as well? Think about it.

Terri   Yes, Ken still calls when he says he'll call. Thank you for asking. Thanks for remembering that. And for remembering his name.

Mme Wyatt   Did I really? Did I truly say that the only immutable rule of marriage was that a man never leaves his wife for an older woman? And do I still think so? I have no idea. I do not remember that I believed this. I am not certain that I know very much, finally.

Ellie   Do I feel conned? By Stuart? Yes and no. The weird thing is, I feel more conned by Gillian. Something in her attitude. Like, you can have Stuart for a bit, be my guest, because I can get him whenever I want him. Maybe she didn't even bother to think that. But she ought to have, oughtn't she?

Gillian   That's the stupidest question I've ever heard. *Me?*

   Yes, Oliver attacked me ten years ago.

   Yes, Stuart attacked me recently.

   But I provoked Oliver deliberately. Whereas I didn't provoke Stuart. There's no connection between the two incidents. None at all.

   It's a very stupid term, in my opinion. Professional victim.

Oliver   [*declined to answer any further questions*]

Stuart   I'm very glad you asked that. Personally I use Carnaroli – that's what the Milanese use. Or Vialone Nano. That's more Venetian. Let me give you a tip. If it's a springtime risotto, asparagus or *primavera*, say, then at the end, instead of the normal tablespoonful of butter, I use *crème fraîche*. It sort of lightens it up. Just an idea.

20: What Do You Think?

Gillian   There's something I haven't told you. Something Stuart said.

When we were making love – no, when he was raping me – no, let's say when we were having sex – and I was trying to tell him it was a bad idea, I was going to say something about Oliver, but for some reason I couldn't mention his name. So I found myself saying – and I know it must have sounded peculiar – something like 'My husband's sleeping upstairs.'

'No,' Stuart said. He stopped fucking me for a moment and looked at me quite seriously, but also aggressively. '*I'm* your husband. I've always been your husband. You're my wife.'

'Stuart,' I said. I mean, he wasn't some old fundamentalist with a beard. This was us, here, now.

'I'm your husband,' he repeated. 'You may be Oliver's mistress, but you're *my wife*.'

Then he carried on fucking me.

Don't you find that scary?

Oliver   Plan A (forgive the lapse into Stuartese). Marry Mrs Dyer. Change name to Dyer in tribute. Support her like that ripe fruit in the hand until the stalk parts tenderly from the branch. Inherit her house. Live across the road from the newly remarried Hugheses. Try not to be a nuisance. The noble self-effacement worthy of Roncesblah-blah. Celebrate reversibility – you recall it was my watch-word?

Plant a new monkey-puzzle tree. Speed its growth, and let it mask the outside world before my own medlar-moment arrives.

Stuart   You meet someone, you get to know them, you like them, they like you, you go to bed together. Then – at that point, or the next morning, or looking back – things become clearer, don't they? Whether it's likely to be once more out of curiosity or politeness on both sides (or never again out of politeness on both sides), or whether it's going to be something to last the season, or whether – just possibly – it could run and run. It normally becomes clearer in your mind.

I suppose you could say that the present circumstances aren't exactly normal. Yes, you could say that again.

Gillian   I don't believe in abortion. That's to say, leaving aside things that happen in war zones and so on, I don't believe in most of the abortions that take place in the world. I don't contest any woman's right, but I do contest the wisdom. It's a big thing to bring a child into the world, but it's a bigger thing to stop one coming into it. I know all the arguments, but the decision, it seems to me, is always made at a place beyond argument. The same place where all the other decisions about things like love and faith are made.

So if all goes well – and I am beginning to push the age limit – I'll be having Stuart's child. The start of that sentence doesn't fit with the end, somehow.

And it's no solution to go to bed with Oliver as soon as possible and pretend it's his.

Could I say I was having an affair with person or persons unknown? Blame it on the non-existence of our sex-life? Except that I work at home and Oliver's been housebound too recently. He knows what I do. My time is accounted for.

He'll guess, of course. And I won't deny it.

Oliver   Plan B. Oliver of Roncesblahblah was not, I trow, famous for self-effacement. Honour propels me. Sound the mighty conch and onward into battle! Smite the uncircumcised! (A point heretofore unconsidered. Surprised you didn't pop that one during your recent inquisition. Stuart – does he retain his sacred halo, his fleshly prepuce, or not? Cavalier or Roundhead, what do you think? [*Me? Moi?* As I say, you've missed your chance. Though if you like – and Oliver is so *triste*ly short of funds nowadays – we could meet *afterwards*, and you can pay me to show you. Yes, lay my todger among the drachmae. Take a polaroid. Entitle it: How Things Work.]) So – into battle? Fight for what is mine by right, honour, and the joining of hands. Woo and win again. Protect my lineage. What do you think?

Stuart   What did I say about wanting?

I said, 'Nowadays I know what I want and I don't waste time with what I don't want.' I made it sound so clear-cut, didn't I? And for a lot of the time it is, or has been. But only, I realise, with simple things, unimportant things. You want them, and you get them. Or you don't.

With important things, though . . . Wanting may lead to getting, but getting isn't the end of the story. It just throws up a new set of questions. Remember when Oliver said his business plan was to win the Nobel Prize? More chance of him winning a triple rollover on the Lottery, I think you'll agree. But just imagine, for a moment, that he got what he wanted. Do we think that would solve his problems and he'd live happily ever after? I don't think so. You could say that it's easier never to get, just to want. Except that a life of wanting and not getting can be incredibly painful. Believe me.

Or am I just avoiding the issue? Talking about 'wanting things', and not even mentioning Gillian's name?

Sophie   Stuart's my Daddy and Daddy's Marie's Daddy, which is one of the things Daddy's Down in the Dumps about. (We haven't found a grown-up word for it yet.)

So maybe the answer's for Dad and Mum to have another baby together. Then it would be two to one.

Hey, isn't that brilliant? Brilliant. What do you think?

Gillian   It didn't work, did it? That's the truth of it. Ten years ago, I engineered a scene which I thought would set Stuart free. But it seems to have had the opposite effect. I hoped he would see that my life with Oliver was nothing to be envied and this would get him off the hook. Do you know, when he first went to America, he used to send me these huge bunches of flowers. Anonymously. I made friends with the delivery company, gave them a story about a possible stalker, and they confirmed that they were all authorised from Washington. And Stuart, needless to say, was the only person I knew there. And obviously Oliver knew. We just never discussed it. Then we moved to France, and still he tracked us down. So I arranged this scene in the street, when I knew Stuart would be watching. But I totally miscalculated, because it must have made Stuart want to rescue me. And all those years I thought he was fine, off on his own, safe, the wounds healed.

If, instead, he'd seen the truth – that Oliver and I were happy – as we were, then – would that have set him free? Would he have had a completely different life? Might he never have come back? It's that unanswered, unanswerable question about the lives we could have led and didn't; the abandoned alternatives, the forgotten choices. What do you think?

Oliver   Plan C. What did Dr Robb tell me? Yes – feeling that you're not going to get better is all part of the depression. Well, I would agree, though my textual gloss would be different from hers. Back in my student days I had bar-stool acquaintance with a young doctor, recently qualified. One quaffing eve he was of doleful aspect. A senior sawbones had that afternoon instructed him – now that he was a grown-up whitecoat – to convey the terminally bad news to the assembled family of a patient who was even then being nibbled, gnawed and fatally munched by the rodent cancer. My chum had never played the fatal messenger before and was unversed in the ways of diplomacy; and yet, it seems to me, he was a veritable Sir Henry Wotton in the way he told the stricken family that their beloved hubby, sire and loinchild was certain to croak. What exactly did you say, I enquired, and his words to me still echo down the decades. 'I told them that he wasn't going to get better.'

So young, and yet so wise! Are we any of us going to get better? Certainly not in the sense the philosophers understand. Nor in the sense of The Men Who Guess. The feeling that you're not going to get better is indeed part of the depression – but which part? For Dr Robb it is a symptom, for Oliver the cause. We are none of us going to get better, so why send honest medical ambassadors to lie abroad for the good of their country? Plan C merely consists of acknowledging the facts as they are. We are all in the same boat, it is just that some admit we are holed below the waterline, while others bend their oblivious backs and pull on the oars until the rowlocks glow.

Look at that cliché. Worse, at the doomed attempt to give it life. What a disgrace. Shame on you, Ollie my sweet. But then, in self-defence, how appropriate. What are our lives but doomed attempts to revive a cliché?

Yes, that's Plan C.

Plan A, Plan B. Plan C: Would You Rather?

Stuart   What I mean by 'more complicated' is this. While I was away all those years, the Gill I carried around with me – quite literally in the case of that photo everyone seems a bit obsessed by – was the Gill I knew back then, the one I'd fallen in love with. That's normal, isn't it? And when I came back, I said to myself, she hasn't changed a bit. I mean, she's got the girls, and she does her hair in a different way, and she's put on a bit of weight, and doesn't wear any of the clothes I remember, and is living in reduced circumstances, but to me she was exactly the same. Is she? Maybe I just don't want to admit that all these years of living with Oliver might have changed her. Exposure to his ways and thoughts and second-rate opinions. We're talking ADIs and MRLs, as I said. Is it unrealistic to assume she's still the same woman I fell in love with? After all, I've changed in the intervening years. And so, as I pointed out when we said hello, have you.

The sex didn't make things clearer. On the contrary, it made me realise I've been deceiving myself by assuming it's an open-and-shut case, that I've always loved Gill, always have and always will. Because the Gill of that sentence is the Gill of twelve years ago: that's what I know I'll always love. Always. Hard drive, as I said: beefy men with sledgehammers would have to smash up my heart. But what about the Gill of today? Will I have to fall in love with her all over again? Or am I halfway there already? A quarter? Three-quarters? Have you been in this sort of situation yourself? I'm a bit in the dark. I suppose the ideal solution would be to discover that although we've both changed, we've been developing in parallel directions, so that we haven't 'grown apart', as they say, even if we've been apart. And then – better still, and the biggest If – to find that she could come to love me again. Or – even better yet – to love me more this time round. Tell me, am I dreaming?

Now that it seems there's an outside chance of getting back what I once had, part of me is beginning to wonder how much I want it. When things were impossible, they were clearer. Perhaps I'm just scared. After all, the stakes feel so much higher now. I suppose the key question is, could Gillian come to love me again?

What do you think?

Gillian   Does Stuart love me? Still? Really? As he said? That's the key question.

What do you think?

Mme Wyatt   Don't ask me anything. Something will happen. Or nothing. And then, one after the other, over a long period of time, we'll all die. You may die first, of course.

So as for me, I will wait. For something to happen. Or for nothing to happen.